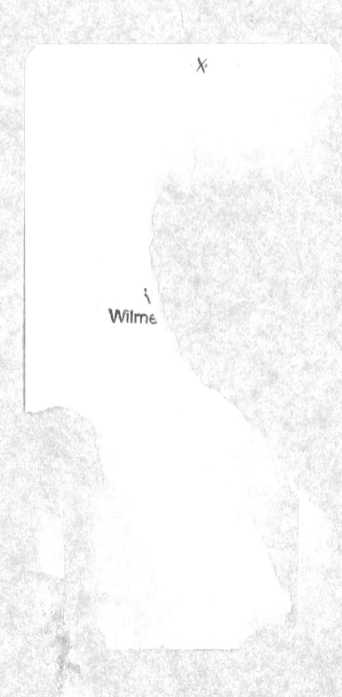

X.

Wilme

IN THE CREVICE OF TIME

JOHNS HOPKINS:
POETRY AND FICTION

JOHN T. IRWIN, GENERAL EDITOR

IN THE

CREVICE

OF TIME

NEW AND COLLECTED
P O E M S

JOSEPHINE
JACOBSEN

THE JOHNS HOPKINS UNIVERSITY PRESS   BALTIMORE AND LONDON

This book has been brought to publication with the generous assistance
of the Albert Dowling Trust.

The Johns Hopkins University Press
2715 North Charles Street
Baltimore, Maryland 21218-4319
The Johns Hopkins Press Ltd., London

ISBN 0-8018-5116-5

Library of Congress Cataloging-in-Publication Data
will be found at the end of this book. ·

A catalog record for this book is available from the British Library.

Some of these poems first appeared in the following volumes and periodicals: *The American
Voice, The Atlantic, Commonweal, Epoch, Grand Street, The Johns Hopkins Review, The Kenyon
Review, Maryland Poetry Review, Midwest, The Nation, New Letters, The New Republic, The
New Yorker, Ploughshares, Poetry, Poetry Newsletter, Poetry Newspaper, Prairie Schooner, Saturday
Review, Second Rising, Southern Poetry, Tri-Quarterly, Vantage,* and *Yankee.* Grateful acknowl-
edgment is made for permission to reprint.

For Eric

The author wishes to express her great gratitude to the MacDowell Colony and to Yaddo, where a number of the poems were written; and to Charlotte Blaylock and Dr. Evelyn Prettyman for invaluable assistance in assembling this manuscript.

Contents

PART THREE   1965 ▪ 1970

PART FIVE   1975 ▪ 1994

1 9 3 5

1 9 5 0

Lines to a Poet

Be careful what you say to us now.
The street-lamp is smashed, the window is jagged,
There is a man dead in his blood by the base of the fountain.
If you speak
You cannot be delicate or sad or clever.
Some other hour, in a moist April,
We will consider similes for the budding larches.
You can teach our wits and our fancy then;
By a green-lit midnight in your study
We will delve in your sparkling rock.
But now at dreadful high noon
You may speak only to our heart,
Our honor and our need:
Saying such things as, "See, she is alive . . ."
Or "Here is water," or "Look behind you!"

Non Sum Dignus

This Sabbath, as all others, finds
The building hushed for love of God,
Save where the thin man, counting, winds
His watch, and children creak and nod

In crowded pews. The money chinks
Discreetly in the moving plate;
Through the stained glass the sunlight winks
On Adam at the Garden-gate.

Hands reach for gloves and rosaries—
"The Mass is ended" comes so soon—
Beyond the window butterflies
Sprinkle with white the burning noon.

The ancient usual retreat
Takes down the steps the scattering horde;
Adam again has met defeat,
Has missed connections with the Lord.

But where the altar-candles die
Waits God, and in a corner prays
The last of heroes who will try
The Gate again in seven days.

Winter Castle

I   THIS THEN SHALL BE OUR APRIL . . .

This then shall be our April—this black heap
Lifting its stones from these forgotten snows;
The winds of these white slopes shall weave our sleep
For summer breezes, and the owl that goes
Silent and swift from turret to black bole
Shall serve as nightingale. And in the storm,
When torches die and tempest shakes the soul
And branches crack and only love is warm,
This rage shall be our sweets of spring. No birds
Shall sing at these cold casements, and the day
Will bring no sun to thaw such ice—but words
There shall be spoken here and in such way
Not all July as these shall burn so bright
Within this sorrowful and savage night.

II   LET BE; ENOUGH . . .

Let be; enough; I am not yours tonight
To touch and take. Though we lie neighbored here,
A bitter wind has put the crows to flight
Seeking rare shelter and the stars cut clear
Upon the frosted earth. I have escaped
In some uncommon way through the thick walls,
And I am many-minded, diverse-shaped:
I am the horses, hay-warmed in the stalls,
The snow-sagged spruces, and the starving hare
Coursing the slopes of snow. It is not well
That you should hold my body with this care
And tell me things, as I were here to tell,
While I am distant, hunting in the chill
With wolves that run upon the hungry hill.

III KNOWING YOUR BODY . . .

Knowing your body and the lines of it,
Knowing a portion of your heart, at worst,
There is a country in your mind unlit
By any torch of mine. I have a thirst
Tonight to spy its wells, hunger to touch
My fingers to its fruit, desire to trace
Its dark horizons and to climb and clutch
Its dizzy goat-paths where the sharp winds race
And flying clouds are close; and if my lust
For finding things bring me a bitter view,
Why, I am one whom danger never thrust
Away from her so sharply as she drew,
Our hands together, on the cruel ground
I shall stand steadfastly, and make no sound.

Escape in Ice

We have forgotten weather, by virtue of the protecting mass
Of wall. We may remark the voice of January in the eaves,
Or a blue-and-green May day, blowing over, beyond the glass,
But they are neither kind nor cruel, the ice, the leaves.

On a day this winter our lives were minutely altered—
The lanes were bright and smooth as the clicking branches of trees,
All was touched by a giant finger—the inexorable rhythm faltered,
And ice and wind became larger, and real, and we were captive of these.

Men kept at home, there was no school, the children curled
By the fire and people spoke in a special voice;
The tides and winds and seasons of the ancient world
Were again in power for a moment, and the heart could in secret rejoice

In the glittering pause, in the old recurrence, that discovers
To men nervous with power, the helpless escape. The fierce weather
Is master; all life is in the small warm room. And the lovers
Stare through blind windows and laugh, and come together.

Terrestrial

This day was made of dust,
The bright and lovely
And utterly perishing—
Nothing that we could trust, nothing worth cherishing.

No skeleton to stay and whiten,
No soul to escape—
The word was *never,*
Nothing like *love,* to frighten; dust, lost forever.

Moss, rainbow rock, fall apart,
The cold pools vanish
Without resurrection.
The alien human heart, strange to perfection

Understands this, its own:
Not past, not future,
Not truth, to enmesh us—
This was our dust alone, O ours, O precious.

For Wilfred Owen

This day, this night, should be familiar to you,
These sounds, these faces, this red mud and glare;
Again is served, upon the board that knew you,
The ugly feast at which you took your share.

The skeletons at ease beneath the crosses
Are unconcerned with diving Messerschmitts,
Impervious to estimated losses
And unambitious of director hits.

They, safe as you, ignore delirium;
This time your lips escape the bitter ration,
And the sick stumbling men whose lips are dumb
Go scatheless from your terrible compassion.

Spring, Says the Child

There are words too ancient to be said by the lips of a child—
Too old, too old for a child's soft reckoning—
Ancient, terrible words, to a race unreconciled:
Death, spring . . .

The composite heart of man knows their awful age—
They are frightening words to hear on a child's quick tongue.
They overshadow, with their centuries' heritage,
The tenderly young.

Death, says the child, *spring,* says the child, and *heaven* . . .
This is flesh against stone, warm hope against salt sea—
This is all things soft, young, ignorant; this is even
Mortality.

For Those Who Have Not Eaten the Apple

The unclosing flowers are inflexible and have yielded nothing;
At the tree's base the hairy grass is strong and green,
And there is an ignorance of guilt, of weariness; a breathing
Of uncomplicated air, as in some pre-apple Eden.

This is innocence: it dwells in savage children,
In unreflecting men cleaning the valves, in the birds'
Tempestuous blood; it cannot understand the hidden
Meaning of good. It is too fresh for the word's age.

This is alluring: it is the scathelessness of the new,
The stiffness of virgin cloth, the motion of young men;
It is the gift of the child, it is cold and clear, like dew,
Calling not for admiration but certainly for envy.

Tango

The pulse of
Violin
Is counting, and the beat
Will draw them in
On geometric feet.

This is here, like God, is precise in its every act,
This is honest as numbers, as numbers it meets the advance;
This is the always-sought, the unyielding fact,
What of their own they can offer must be shaped to this dance.

Sharp as
A sword
The pattern laid together,
The stern
Accord,
The drifting, double feather.

This is the plan they could never never find,
The formula, Exactly so shall the thing be done.
Life would not tell them this, but now, combined,
In perfection of knowledge they move, they are two, they are one.

The body
Learns
The paradise of laws,
The perfect
Turns,
The perfect, balanced pause.

They have found it now. While the music lasts, this is more
Than skill, than rhythm, than movement, than all of these;
More than shadows above the space of the shining floor,
More than a woman and man. This is justice, is peace.

This cancels
Fear,
To pause, to close, to cross;
The sum
Is here—
No loss, no fraction's loss.

Let Each Man Remember

There is a terrible hour in the early morning
When men awake and look on the day that brings
The hateful adventure, approaching with no less certainty
Than the light that grows, the untroubled bird that sings.

It does not matter what we have to consider,
Whether the difficult word, or the surgeon's knife,
The last silver goblet to pawn, or the fatal letter,
Or the prospect of going on with a particular life.

The point is, they rise; always they seem to have risen
(They always will rise, I suppose) by courage alone.
Somehow, by this or by that, they engender courage,
Courage bred in flesh that is sick to the bone.

Each in his fashion, they compass their set intent
To rout the reluctant sword from the gripping sheath,
By thinking, perhaps, upon the Blessed Sacrament,
Or perhaps by coffee, or perhaps by gritted teeth.

It is indisputable that some turn solemn or savage,
While others have found it serves them best to be glib,
When they inwardly lean and listen, listen for courage,
That bitter and curious thing beneath the rib.

With nothing to gain, perhaps, and no sane reason
To put up a fight, they grip and hang by the thread,
As fierce and still as a swinging threatened spider.
They are too brave to say, It is simpler to be dead.

Let each man remember, who opens his eyes to that morning,
How many men have braced them to meet the light,
And pious or ribald, one way or another, how many
Will smile in its face, when he is at peace in the night.

Laurentides

I   VIRGIN IN GLASS

The little Virgin, fitted out in white
Behind the glass
Set in the center of the cross's height,
Inhabits quietly her novel plight,
Far from the Mass.

Above her head the symbols of the Line—
Carved arrow,
Pincers and hammer—lie within the sign
Of a thorn circle, cut in blunt design,
Wooden and narrow.

Below her sheltered perch the jagged rocks
Girdle the cross;
Serenely pink-cheeked in her little box
She gazes wisely on the winter fox,
The summer moss.

She was installed with wreaths and holiday
In bright July,
Blessed by the priest, pleasured by noise and play;
Priest, games and summer come and go away.
Her scrutiny

Stays to encounter the uplifted gaze
Of kneeling men,
Of children such a doll can still amaze,
Of women come to bargain or to praise.
In blizzards, when

A moose, encouraged by the private snow
Treads somberly
Across her vision, she will meet his slow
And doubtful look, before he turns to go
Not wholly free.

II BY THE ROCK

Search in the quiet of this motionless spot .
Past the submerged brown stone, the pallid knot
Of streaked thin lake-grass; seek beyond the small
And desolate leaf sequestered since its fall
In shallow water. Furry mosses lock
The rotting stick in growth. Here is the rock,
Bronzed, ridged and tinted. This shall be to you
Refuge in thought—rock clung to by the blue
And red-rust lichen, glided over by
The flickering fish's circular pop eye,
Spotted with fleeing shadow from the wing
Of dragonfly. The ripples shivering
Beneath the wind do not perturb its face,
Its silent aqueous life. Remark this place.

III THIS HOUSE

This house is a room—divided, but still a room—
Shining by light. The floor hard-stung by the broom,
The china swan outswelling with shaggy bloom,

And especially the walls, give back a rich response
To the pulse of the sheltered flame that beats in its sconce—
The walls of silk-smooth birch that were growing once.

There is almost no sound. The chipmunks are in the roof
And they cling and peer down, but their family life is aloof
As the moose that leaves print in the mold of his chiseling hoof.

Outside is the night. Outside the forests begin,
With claw and fur, and the lakes, with webbed foot and fin;
The walls, the swan and the breathing lamp are within.

Now the rubbish is torn away, and the clogging vines
From the single plant are wrenched, and the warm light shines
On the pattern of life, lifting spare and unalterable lines.

In Isolation

When at a desperate plight
His sentience quits its mesh
To taste the acrid fright
Within the alien flesh,

To know the separate pain
Which is no piece of his,
Almost a man may gain
Identity in this.

Almost he may believe
He has worked miracle
And does in fact conceive
An unfamiliar hell;

Almost he shall descry
The small and dreadful day
From which he cannot fly
Because there is no way;

Almost he has escaped
Ego's lonely law;
Here are two halves, twin-shaped,
Divided by a straw.

Just at identity,
Just as the perfect tone,
Suddenly he is free—
Suddenly it is lost . . . gone.

Once more descends the chill
The healthy life has shunned
Where move in secret still
The sad and moribund.

From artificial care
Fostered beyond its scope,
Goes up the stranger's prayer,
The insulated hope.

February Midnight

No sheltered ear can miss,
Though stalwart be the wall,
At midnight such as this,
The homeless faint footfall.

The kindly man shall sigh
And feed the friendly flame
And valiantly deny
The small and fierce shame;

The poet's heart shall burn
Until he form a verse
When he shall sigh and turn
And slumber none the worse;

The woman warm in love
Shall find her mind possessed
Now by the rigor of
An uninvited guest,

And sharply start away
From what she might discover
And seek in mute dismay
The body of her lover.

Only the hermit's breath
Frosted upon the air,
Incognizant of death
And conqueror of despair,

Through poverty's sweet ease
Immune from pity's rod,
Shall hold in scatheless peace
Its intercourse with God.

Death and the Turtle

The turtles in the big green bowl are reduced by one;
A turtle climbed out, got lost, is disappeared.
A meticulous search has not found her, she is woefully gone.
Off she crept—the small tail protruding, the small head upreared.

Three days hope was held; but it has vanished. Securely
She may have tucked herself in her shell; unbidden
Came someone who had watched her foolhardy departure. Surely
Death found the turtle, wherever she may have hidden.

Now in her small lost body, under her painted shell
He is entered the house, and it is touched with a curious illness;
With no matter what laughter and noise, what pretense all is well,
We move, little and strange, at the heart of a present stillness.

Man and the Lion

The yellow lion shakes the ground—
Hunting the range which is his choice—
By the great pulse of his profound
And savage voice.

But man confronts, with halted stride
Of twiggy legs, the hot eyeballs
Of the caged cat, and notes with pride
That its gaze falls.

The golden lion of the sun
Staring across the lucent sky
Makes no attempt to catch and stun
The human eye.

Yet, as the mole which shelters in
The grubby and protective dark,
We burrow, when the hunt begins,
Lest we be mark

For the terrible light. How can our spirit
Endure this overheaping measure
Of shame, until we shall inherit
Celestial pleasure

To watch the sun appease his wrath
With glut of stars—the lovely Seven,
The moon—as he crosses on his path
The lit heaven?

"It's a Cold Night," Said Coney to Coney

"It's a cold night," said coney to coney
Deep in the burrow, deep in the ground.
Glass and flame and the fat clock wound,
"It's a cold night," said crony to crony.

"It's a cold night," said gull to gull,
"Over the water to rock and hover."
"The sea is between and the moon is full
And it's a cold night," said lover to lover.

"It's a cold night for soldiers, locks and stocks,
And the moon round for hunter's joy!
Dig down deeper," said fox to fox.
"It's a cold night," said boy to boy.

For Any Member of the Security Police

I

Let us ask you a few questions, without rancor,
In simple curiosity, putting aside
Our reactions or the rising of our gorge,
As a child asks, How does it work? As premise:

Some limitations you admit: sound-proofing
Is never perfect, hints rise from any cellar;
There are a—very—few for whom reshaping
Must be abandoned for that catch-all, death.

The capitulation-point (call it X^2)
In very strong young men, well-fed and finicky,
Is sometimes unbelievably delayed.
Most are much easier: women they love,

The children from their bodies' seed, are garden-paths
To the objective. And humiliation
After the first betrayal, serves as breach
So that all others follow fairly freely.

We haven't yet discussed the top success,
The mind's invasion; that fierce citadel
Proverbially adamant to rack and fire,
To conjuration—even sometimes to love,

Now, by a postern-door, all solved so simply.
Nothing more formidable than a needle,
A pellet; the kindly country-doctor's tools.
Now, with this data in mind, if you could tell us . . .

II

Is there routine in this, like unlocking the desk
And running through the Baskets, In and Out,
Uncovering the typewriter: Memo to Miss Prout;
How was our average on yesterday's task?

The season must sometimes be April, fair beyond fiction,
The inner crocus, enamel; the apple-trees
Fierce with fragrance and strength. You must move among these
In the common lot. Are you dogged by a minor friction?

When in at your window starlight is spilt
From the midnight sky and you, still watcher, see
The moon in silence pass each boundary,
The moon which never will acknowledge guilt,

When your two hands, fresh from their late employ,
Touch in the dark your lover's body, after;
When in the first hot sun climbs her clear laughter,
Do you meet the simplicity of joy?

And when the ambiguous bird in the dark meadow
Cries out an undecipherable message,
And utter stillness is the moment's presage
When there shall bend above you a chill shadow,

Then are you lonely only as all are lonely
Leaving the loved and known, or do you see
A small, unnatural eternity
Shaped otherwise, and fashioned for you only?

Mississippi Anatomy

This land is red, its body is colored of blood,
It is lonely and red,
Only pines spring up. From this barren and scarlet mud
Indifference is bred.

These stretches will form no alliance with starlight or noon;
With a sullen glow
This repulses the sun, it refuses the moon
And is ignorant of snow.

It proffers no proof of its nurture, no cornfield, no spire,
Not a dog, not a cart;
Silent, it draws with confused and reluctant desire
The inscrutable heart.

PART TWO

1 9 5 0

1 9 6 5

Cul de Sac

In the grassplot's center was a bed of red roses,
A circle in a pear; round-eyed and fragrant
The great tame blossoms loaded the noon
With pleasure; the grass sparkled under the sprinkler;
The trees ranked black, banking the driveway;
The ferns sprang, still. A treetrunk came alive

With a cautious coon face cocked round the bole.
It watched the brightness and Erlend
Who held his hoe in wonder: Enemy
Watched watching enemy. Sidelong
The raccoon in silence without fear or cunning
Came down and shambled into the sun.

Out of the woods and the shade and the silence
It crept toward the sunny boy on the grass
Gaudy with drops. It crouched and lifted—
Anxious and silent in the blaze
Of sun and water and roses—its head
To what it should have known to be deadly.

Erlend got food in a white cracked bowl.
The raccoon ate it, using his hands,
His sinewy fingers; but he would not drink.
He wove over to Erlend's feet and stared.
His eyes stared up, dark from the dark fur,
He stared up in silence but urgently.

The rest was ugly and rapid. He was mad.
He stiffened, upright, water came from his mouth,
His mask contorted and he fell; got up;
Reared stiff, and fell, got up, and ran
Around. Shots ended the dumb-show suffering,
The raccoon was quiet in a bloody ruff.

It was insanity that brought him
Silent from the normal wood's hostility
Onto the bright unnatural grassplot,
Pigeon-toed, shambling, aping a pet;
But he was neither sane nor degraded;
He came from shadows to the blazing day.

He came to the devil-angels of his myth,
Crept to the glare of danger to be saved;
Alone, a crazy alien in the trees,
Was drawn to break bread in a travesty
Of friendship. The calendar and woods forgot him.
Not so the human who succored and shot him.

Variations on Variety

I   COMIC

Conservative heart, outdone by all upheaval,
Let solid laughter, greeting the emergence
Of stooge and comic from the wings, set free
Your fear from troubled dreams of anarchy:
These point the norm by patter of divergence.

Semple and Simple, in costume as in concept,
Bank on the ancient timing of surprise:
The strength of midget, lewdness of duenna,
The slipping pants, the skin of the banana,
Rest on the pattern where all these are lies.

To a thousand minds, the traveling-salesman-gag
Supports the marble niche of chastity—
(Presupposition of the two-a-day)
As each round penny of the juggler's pay
Supports the implacable rule of gravity.

II   TIGHT-ROPE WALKER

The bright-check suited
Walks—our hope—
To music, muted,
The vibrant rope.

In a sliding dance
He moves to measure;
Our life, in balance,
Our swaying treasure.

With red-glow gaze
Watch the evil three:
Vertigo, praise
And gravity.

To their shame, to their rage
At the other side
He has leaped to the stage,
He is bowing, our pride.

This is sweet, which we shared:
He has justified men;
We are puny, we dared,
We have conquered again.

III SISTER ACT

Red, blue and green, the Murphy sisters sing, and interstellar space
Has not frightened their scintillant, sequined trio from the sycophant
      microphone
That dulcetly magnifies murmurs; and they are—heads together, casual
      arm about waist—
On a stage in a city in a country on a continent, superbly at home.

Street-lamp, façade and alley, slum, urban garden and plaza and
      boulevard
Lie, wrapped and reassuring, round them, then Maryland hills and water
And wide wide to the west rolling under the moonlight that enormous
      word
America; but a word like *oceans* is bigger and colder and weightier.

The hanging hemispheres, the pendant water caught back from its fall,
· Stand them in stead; three undismayed, not given to brooding vainly;
The baby-spot clasps them, so that the spinning, tiny star in its well
Of black winds rushing through space, of nothing and nowhere and
        none, shall not make them lonely.

Green, blue and red, they are able to take an encore with an ending soft
        and high,
For terror will not open upon them like a door with an oiled hinge.
They can bow like jonquils—for the mind will not step to their shoul-
        der, and succinct and wicked, betray
The device spread over thin space, the tissue-paper between the foot and
        the plunge.

Explorer

He traveled, traveled in the human climate,
Avid of accent, custom, idiom—
Each port a promise, and the leaf and loam
Vibrant with wonder to communicate:

Tubbed trees, close tables and the coffee-hum—
Jacques' well-paved boulevard, shellacked with noon;
Bon mot, the blood, and repartee, the bone,
And for the soul, a neat and abstract sum.

Sweet as the stealing of a theme forgotten,
Emma's June pasture, where opinions browse
Under paternal skies, like faithful cows
Kept for their comfort, and the daisies fatten.

Highways of habit; naiveté like a garden,
And the heart's jungle-paths; the lonely fear
To be traversed like a blue glacier;
And ego, for the dungeon's jaded warden.

O drums, bells, water! Mirror-bright oasis,
All green to greet and lavish to the dry,
Flashing and fertile to the amorous eye—
Sand is the substance, sand the dreadful basis;

Restless as grief, storm-shaped and wind-tormented,
Stinging and sterile in its lonely rage—
Salute the courage of the brief mirage
Despair and ingenuity invented.

Through club with careful membership to offer,
Each locker-room more opulent and duller;
Through orient palace, all delight and color,
Where everything save pity gleams in coffer;

Over the herb-plot of the artist's ground,
Past the old battlefield whereon the spirit
Won, in another month, a certain merit,
And died, a little later, of its wounds.

But in the crowded loneliness all lost,
With every boat and train a nightmare trap,
He suddenly won back to his unique hope—
Love's moonlight-laden apple-boughs at rest.

Fire Will Not Change

Fire wakes with a burst in the tower of leaf—
(Leaves and fire are ever the dead and the quick)
Distorted, like flies in death—(they were flexible, green)
Leaves go on the lizard-tongues that leap and lick.

But being an element, fire will not change,
It harbors another thing on which it has fed.
The bodies fly up: the host which went by the flame,
Each terrified body crowned by its sentient head.

As praise to the teakwood profile, the cold stone mouth,
Out of old nights, in jungle, on temple-altar;
As medicinal scourge to the wilful ailing soul
While parchment pardon was raised, should the devil falter;

The Parsee widow, fifteen, and enamoured of breath;
The crone who kept only one cow, but whose eye could bewitch;
The man of our nation and day, in the piney growth,
We threw back as he crept from the core of the burning pitch.

In the gust of the April flames see how they blow;
Their voices lift, up streams their forking hair . . .
Rake the innocent leaves, pile the pure brush. You invoke
Fire unchanged. Always its host is there.

Fiddler Crab

The fiddler crab fiddles, glides and dithers,
dithers and glides, veers; the stilt-eyes
pop, the legs prance, the body glides, stops,
the front legs paw the air like a stallion,
at a fast angle he veers fast, glides, stops,
dithers, paws.

The water is five shades of blue. On the rocks
of the reefridge the foam yelps leaping, the big rock
here is glutted with breathers under their clamped clasp,
scarab shapes and tiny white and black whorls.
The lacy wink lapses, behind it the black lustre
lapses and dulls.

I saw the fiddler crab veer, glide, prance,
dither and paw, in elliptical rushes
skirt the white curve and flatten on the black
shine. He veered in a gliding rush
and up to piled sand and into a trembling hole
where grains fell past him.

I imitated him with my five fingers, but not well.
Nothing else moved on the sand. He came out.
My hand cast a shadow. He raised a notch and ran
in tippity panicky glide to the wave's wink.
Each entirely alone on his beach; but who
is the god of the crabs?

On the balcony over the rocks two hours later
The Spanish-Chinese boy brought him to show.
His stilted eyes popped over three broken legs
but he ran with the rest of them over the edge
and died on the point of the drop down
twenty feet.

So it is simple: he can be hurt
and then he can die. In all his motions
and marine manoeuvres it was easy to miss
on the sand how I should know him and he me
and what subject matter we have in common.
It is our god.

Ballad of Henry, Bridegroom

Henry of England could pray or roister,
He had power and youth and some acumen;
The world, indeed, was Henry's oyster—
But this is the ballad of man and woman.
He was strong and proud and his wrath was red.
Comes the day when the quick are the dead,
Christ have mercy when we are sped.

Catherine's pride was tortured and white
But stiff as the bone of Aragon—
Alien queen who could suffer and fight
But never could rear an English son.
"One flesh till death," Spanish Catherine said.
Comes the day when the quick are the dead,
Christ have mercy when we are sped.

The barge was burnished, the roof was gold,
The cannon spoke for the bright newcomer;
Pelted with blossoms, fair and bold
Ann rode the burning Thames of summer.
Nan Bullen had a shining head.
Comes the day when the quick are the dead,
Christ have mercy when we are sped.

Jane, you followed a bloody ghost
Who had been loved, if kings can love;
Henry at last lay by your dust,
Whatever this wish of his may prove.
Jane was honest as salt or bread.
Comes the day when the quick are the dead,
Christ have mercy when we are sped.

Anne of Cleves was a sorry sequel
And doubtless a shock to a bridegroom who
Had been told that her beauty knew no equal
And found this something undertrue.
Henry and Anne kept a virgin's bed.
Comes the day when the quick are the dead,
Christ have mercy when we are sped.

Henry's sense of royal decorum
Found Catherine Howard's virtue lax;
Thomas Culpeper, Francis Derham
Paid by the rope, and his queen by the axe.
The three were young and nobly bred.
Comes the day when the quick are the dead.
Christ have mercy when we are sped.

Catherine seemed hardly a name for luck,
Nor this elevation a thing to seek;
Catherine Parr, when the long-due struck,
Your distinction remains unique:
You abode when your master fled.
Comes the day when the quick are the dead,
Christ have mercy when we are sped.

The word that pleased him least, was *wife,*
The word writ deep in his heart was *nation;*
He had lively faith in the afterlife,
Probably mixed with trepidation.
What speech holds the king with these he wed
Now in the day when the quick are the dead?
Christ have mercy when we are sped.

The Innocents

The faces of children turn like sunflowers to death;
With popcorn and attention they defer
To the ditch-dead woman snuffed by the timid cur,
The sudden soldier spinning on the beach,

(Raped from the roses, from the summer-core,
From the cool parlour with the peacock-feathers,
By the dark shrine that miracles all weathers
All oceans and all foreignness to Here.)

The guilty adults watch the faces turn
Uplifted to the toadstool of disaster
That rears before them bigger faster vaster
Than any cautious parent made them learn;

The guilty adults watch with sterile eyes
The peacock-feather vase; locked from the garden
Weep penance for themselves and find no pardon
For this deflowering—and never see

The awkward lady with the queer eye-sockets,
The funny airman dropping like a swallow;
The terrible peacock-eyes that seem to follow,
The striped rage of the monstrous yellowjacket.

Shibboleth

Tonight I saw the marred and frosted moon.
It sat high in the bare sky over
your naked shoulder and the thin rich line
of vineleaves in the green glass bottle.
And instantly here was the curve of the child's arm;
also the dying man drying in his corner
when the truck took the colored crests of bough
with shouts, in the strong autumn ether.
Child was in the bleachers, old man inside the window; bared
sky was around the moon which was frosted and marred.

Four years had shaped the arm to make its mythical curve
melt to the wrist like love:
the diamond blazed, the runner held,
but the fold of the curve drew down the word.
The old man dried in his chair behind glass
to hear them bear away
the colored tops-of-trees the linesmen's truck
shook in shimmers away down his October street.
To the moon's green vine came the trapped man's motionless form,
to the lover's midnight came the curve of the arm.

The desperate Ephraimites cried "Sibboleth!" to the watch;
so cried, and died for the letter.
Now here is Gilead, but here and here your breath
says "Shibboleth"; so says the moony bottle and its vine;
so says the utter curve. But the boughs that vanish and the slow-
dying man drying by glass
say "Shibboleth!" All sibling angels of a password
heard in the midnight room at the point of love.
What angels? Tell me, what angels? The angels of death
and love, to the Gileadites crying "Shibboleth!"

Poet as Mute

For Hans Andersen

Meteor flying and the planets' chime
He, lying like another on mattress and pillow
Hears—as his ear as a shell rings hollow—
Knows—as water is known to the willow—
At midnight, on the turn and shift of time.

Anciently and again ensnared
By the treacherous offer of love and sleep,
Instead, the little mortal feels his shape
Inflated out of scale by savage hope,
Huge with the giant wonder of the word.

He went down to the sea-witch's domain
Wearing the little mermaid's mask:
Treasure washed to wrack and husk,
The ghost of riches distant from the moon.

By the dead seamaid polyps' hands have riven
In terror she passes (bright with bane
The gushing mud, the house of bone)
To sell a tongue for the far chance of heaven,

So that later, when questioned by the handsome prince
"she looked at him very mournfully from her dark
blue eyes, for" (we know) "she could not speak."
Not once upon a time, alas; not once . . .

Now as Eliza, speechless as she spins
(Against enchantment and the fagot
Of troubled king and fierce prelate)
Brothers and princes from the feathers of swans.

Silent in silence she, by graveyard stone
Where hideous the lamias gambol,
Spied on has plucked the stinging nettle
With the eleventh-hour-and-shirt unspun.

But though the great birds assemble in glory, the flame
Will have her, for the flax unfinished,
The shining proof of mail, unfurnished;
Always the youngest brother has the swan's shame.

There is no use expecting the penalty to be lighter,
Nor bells to ring themselves in carols
Nor fagots sprout shoots to spell out morals
In scarlet roses. That was elsewhere and later.

The fire climbs faster, the foam purls over the beach,
The foam purls over the sand, the flames flow faster:
See paradise's mute, the captive master.
Tongueless the seamaid, silent the swans' sister,
Silent our brother in the terrible silence of speech.

Ballad of the Four Saints

Paul, that friend and heir to Christ,
Fought the tiger and the sea.
By the bloody ghost of Stephen
And the stones that set him free,
Paul—with Peter, Mary, Dismas—
Pray for us in charity.

The Magdalene while it was dark
Came to the tomb and found it empty.
By the violent common noon
Of your shame's discovery
Mary—with Paul, Dismas, Peter—
Pray for us in charity.

Peter, crucifixion's clown,
Died with earth where sky should be.
By your tongue of faithless friend
Quicker than the cockerel's cry,
Peter—with Dismas, Mary, Paul—
Pray for us in charity.

Dismas leapt to paradise,
Straight from wood to God went he.
By your clever thievish hand
Later struck upon the tree,
Dismas—with Mary, Paul and Peter—
Pray for us in charity.

Mighty saints who purify
Zealot, traitor, whore and thief,
Peter, Dismas, Mary, Paul
Pray for us in charity.

The Autopsy

At three o'clock their fingers gripped. The sun shot
a big triangle on his sheeted knees. Their fingers
gripped, after argument, in love. His heart beat quiet
invisible and important. Love, like an inept knife
in her hand, had made lacerations but brought no news.

At nine her fingers gripped a pen; his curved
on air, still warm, but faintly. One man let go
her pulse, invisible, important; the other held
the paper still, so she could write her name, and his
who lay with his mysterious heart stopped.

The hall gave a soft sound like a shore or seashell,
the light was aqueous, too. The black floor shone,
the rubber soles went hushing the white shoes.
His door was closed; the other doors ajar.
She wrote his name so they could find his heart.

When she saw him next he was most formal,
stone hands crossed and a familiar coat
buttoned above the wounds the knife had made.
Their knife was better, it had told them something;
hers had not taught her what she wished to know.

The Animals

At night, alone, the animals came and shone.
The darkness whirled but silent shone the animals:
The lion the man the calf the eagle saying
Sanctus which was and is and is to come.

The sleeper watched the people at the waterless wilderness' edge;
The wilderness was made of granite, of thorn, of death,
It was the goat which lightened the people praying.
The goat went out with sin on its sunken head.

On the sleeper's midnight and the smaller after hours
From above below elsewhere there shone the animals
Through the circular dark; the cock appeared in light
Crying three times, for tears for tears for tears.

High in the frozen tree the sparrow sat. At three o'clock
The luminous thunder of its fall fractured the earth.
The somber serpent looped its coils to write
In scales the slow snake-music of the red ripe globe.

To the sleeper, alone, the animals came and shone,
The darkness whirled but silent shone the animals.
Just before dawn the dove flew out of the dark
Flying with green in her beak; the dove also had come.

The Thief

She stole my pencil-case, red leather,
soft, and ten years my friend.
It zipped. Thirty-one pencils in it
long to short, like Aaron's rod
multiplied, held fountains in their spiral.
She was observed: too late I heard;
she sat, sniffled, sniffled, sat, and while I got white paper out
she stole my case.

While I the ninny peered under chair legs
and slapped my pockets, she vanished like a wolf,
the droop-nosed sniffling gray-green bitch!
A torn kodak: (pony, child, and woman
whose light hand lifted beat off the sun from her eyes)
was in the case.
Dust sugared the pony's hooves, the woman squinted in that sun
9000 days ago. I carried it with the pencils
and very precious it was. The thief
dropped her handkerchief over the case, dropped
that in her purse and vanished like a wolf—
the sniffling, shuffling, sadistic thief.

Now my pencils are gone—raped from the paper's touch—
Venus, Faber #2 and a yellow Mogul stub, mongrel-sharp,
that had Monte Alban and a tense noon
by those terrible stones, in its yellow shaft.
The Venus had a thing about the Wallendas
and how pyramids go down, or some
at least, and how when the safe hearts vicariously panicked
the clown called for quiet.
But the mongrel would have bayed
at a flight of birds—not the birds, but the flight—
mechanics of feather and current and the eyes' escape.

Now a snuffling wretch with a mean quick thumb has scooped it—
my scarlet fetish that held possibility:
the dead July, and the pony's dusty twitch and the woman's gesture;
and my performing pencils.
Manège horses, incognito,
straining against a mountain of junk in an August alley,
they will lie, in her service—they will limit
the butcher's guile.

She slipped into an elevator, silly, with her prize
and my poems locked in it.

O Dismas do not ask me to be mild—
to the mean gray wretch, the hag,
the pencil thief!

The Three Children

Else has blown away on the east wind, Richard went away with the wind
    from the west.
Hilary was taken by the wind from the true north.
Still the south wind is here today but the children are gone. Like witches
    or fairytale sons
They came in a three. Like roses or leaves
Or laughter they were gusty. The roses moved and the clear leaves, the
    weather was sunny.
The turn is warm today and the leaves limpid and the roses running.

Else turned somersaults on the granite flags, she had had two years to
    learn whatever she had learned.
She loved fear and a great black dog knocked her down
and licked her rumpled face and she screamed for joy. She waltzed on
    the steep steps and languished through the bannisters.
Richard had thirteen more months and the plans of monsters
Much on his mind. Richard hoped all things while the tricky earth
    turned him over and over.
He was benevolent and wept only at wickedness

And the wind moved his hair and the leaves and roses around him.
    Hilary had a secret or two
Too heavy to touch. He dazzled and dawdled
And understood, with reluctance, thorns and chlorophyll and frost in
    roses and leaves and winds.
He has gone to school to learn simpler things.
The kind gardens of kindergarten have opened their mazes of reas-
    surance to Richard and Else.
Here the winds made the summer of leaves and roses

Blow flying and running about them. The black dog bounded, the
       thunder moved and the hours blew round.
On the tomato-sprayer the cross-bones and skull
Behind the pail in the shed smiled at them, but briefly. In the peaked
       house hung the still bell
And the crayon-man figure was pinned
To sticks and the flames like roses blew in a wind's ghost. The children
       in secret wonder
Watched the faces that watched them.

This is one summer not another. Goodbye, three children never to be
       seen again. *We will come back*
They said, but they will not. They will go so quietly, so completely.
Next summer three strangers whose names were handed like torches
       from the three that went on the north,
East, west winds, from the three who did not could not stay and went
       forever
At no moment with no gesture, irrecoverable as a single petal or a green
       ghost flying, who went
Where?

Goodbye Else, Richard, Hilary, goodbye, goodbye. Goodbye.

Allhallows Party

Down the wet-leaves steps comes the tiger-head
slowly. Five feminine years timid and proud
move the striped stuff toward joy; the limp tail slips behind.

Follows the smaller skull-capped cautious shape,
fraternal, one-footing after the tufted tail-slip.
The terrace swarms with laborious monsters of the maternal mind.

Leaves. Years. Years. Leaves . . . the play will turn more gruff.
There will be treats; and certainly tricks enough.
In some weather she will meet her tiger, his skull will come true.

But they acknowledge that future now and step down, near,
into, the toothy jack-o-lantern light with fear
and courage. Though watched by witches they shall have their due.

Brother Peter Considers Mulroy Drunk under the Rosebush

Let us give praise where praise is due:
the rose sprang single and dew
y; sprang rosy as roses do.

We must announce what we face:
Mulroy lay flat upon his face—
we can see but his surface;

his surface was clogged and lew
d; under the rose rose fern and blue
t, over the rose the wind blew.

This puzzle let us air:
the rose nods on God's air;
Mulroy is Christ's heir.

Poetry to Mulroy's slack p rose,
rose, like the puzzle, g rows—
fragrant, slick-stem, dewy rose.

Mulroy (white, gross and seed
y); bright strong rose, we con cede,
both grew lavish from God's seed.

Clear rose, springing ove
r thick sour flesh, gross g love—
Which is—strange—the be love
d of the Mighty? Strange fierce love.

My Uncle a Child

My uncle, a child in the terrible second coming
tottered, too, but no one cried out for pleasure.

In the nursery of the dead his duplication was faithful: toothless
and without words among the wicked toys of enamel
he teetered with one hand raised in the benediction of paralysis.

The caged and simple thing inside him watched
the parts' disintegration.

Through the window's green spaces came
leaf-sound in motion, the scent of roses
traveled, and airborne tigers landed delicately
on their fragile warped globe. The moon
moved at night, staring, and the clouds
approached in silence and turreted softly away. The earth
spun so unobtrusively that the children
receding like a trick picture (only more slowly)
shuffled and lay and never flew into space.

Inside the nursery each thing grew huge: huge spoon
huge bed-crank; the bed-bars barred
Atlantic and Pacific and the hall,
excluding the restless dragon-glitter of the scaly world.

The children, reprimanded, fed, and prattled to,
called often for the famous visitor.
But when he came it was always for someone else.

At night the nursery slept. My uncle,
the bridegroom of another summer, slept, one hand
on his desire, the pinned bell.
On the nights he lay awake, revenants
smiled in the door but never leapt the lintel.

The simple indivisible watcher waited.
It peered forth without warning, using my uncle's eyes
or expressed itself suddenly in a powerful silence closing his lips.
Ninety Julys were there.
What it selected from the offerings no one could tell.

But love (lips to the grill)
shaped its word (in this latest July, in this imperfect hell never fool-
          proof,
from which escapes could never be eliminated)
and once, in a quick smile of great sweetness,
my total uncle answered.

Instances of Communication

Almost nothing concerns me but communication.
How strange: Up the Orinoco, once, far
up the Orinoco after jungle miles, great flowerheads
looping the treecrests, log-crocodiles, crocodile-logs, bob-haired
Indians naked in praus: a small, hot, town and in an upper dining-room
plashed at by a fountain, cooled by fans, guardian of a menu the size of a
       baby,
speaking six languages, with seven capital cities behind his eyes, a
       headwaiter,
a man, who said without hope, *"And when does your ship sail?"*
       And no one
said to him, *"What are you doing here?"*

In the hall of the inn at Mont Serrat I came out of my room and
"Stand back, stand back!" cried the criada in her softest Spanish, *"the
       bride—*
the bride is coming!" out of her room, down the hall, down to the steps
on her way to the church, to the groom. She was pale, and dark; she
       clouded
the carpet with the mist of her train, she moved by me but turned and
       bent and caught
my fingerbones seeing me like fate, watching the three of her, the old,
       tall, childhood girl,
the darkly seen half-a-thing, and the white bride lost on the point of
       love, and *"Buenas,*
o buenas tardes!" she called into my ear, she crushed my fingers and
       laughed with panic
into my widened eyes and went proudly on whispering
over the hall runner.

I drove five madwomen down a roaring redhot turnpike in a July
noon; the one behind me had a fur ragged coat gathered about her in
        that furnace;
she reached in the horrid insides of a purse and offered me a chocolate,
        liquid
and appalling. *"Look! Look! A bird!"* I cried and flung it over the side
and munched my empty jaws as she turned back, and cried: *"How good!"*
And while the others hummed and cursed, and watched simply,
        suddenly she put
her lips—behind me—to my ear and soft as liquid chocolate came
        purling
the obscene abuse. *"Hush, hush, Laura, hush,"* said the nurse; *"the nice
        lady
likes you!"* Laura did not believe so, and went on softly, slowly, lovingly,
with O such misery of hate.

In frosty Philadelphia the freighter lay and loaded in the Sunday ice.
The great cranes swung, the huge nets grabbed and everything echoed
        from cold:
docks, warehouses, freightrails, ships' prows; everything clicked and
        echoed;
but it was possible to go down the long cold docks over the strange dark
        street under
the dim sky into a cold great warehouse Sunday still, up still cold stairs,
        along
a dark dim cold thin hall through a brown door into a small square
        room with lit
peaky candles and kneeling take—cool, slick, thin, little larger than a
        quarter—
God's blood and body charged with its speech.

Guide for Survivors

First comes the flight, of course. Hope gleams in steel
And lean tracks flash and conjugate the hope:
"I shall escape," "I will escape," even "I am
Escaping"; and the salty prow repeats
In a soft rush, "seascape, safe cape, escape."
Station and quay support him—porter, taxi—
Timid but trustful, through the alien air
To the red reassurance of the lobby.
Pages and aspidistras take him in.
The bedroom door flies back and windowed there
Clash palms, burns bay, felicitous and fresh
With all the tonic tropic of delight.

And only when the blue boy has withdrawn,
His hat on the bed, ice-water at his lips,
Do his eyes meet the eyes in the far corner
Where the squat figure has awaited him.

At this, far too intelligent to flee,
He knows that hope now lies in strategy
And carefully returns to ancient use.
Monsters can mope, and lonely monsters leave.
At midnight, shimmering under falling notes,
Faces of friends like flowers in a rain
Shine fresh as truth, and laughter crests and breaks.
His covert gaze, ranging the rustling room
Finds out no undesired, watching thing;
Best, when the door has closed him in again
With curded smoke and petals dropped on glass,
The place is his. Till, leaning on the mantel,
Who was not there before, regards him, speechless.

Pure terror has him now; now he perceives
The visitor is at home.
                    In the back room
He holds destruction neatly in his palm,
Small, cold and practical, and marvels briefly
Upon how death, that democratic lord,
Can be commanded like a ready lackey
By a crooked finger. But he does not crook it.

Some root of joy, some subterranean pride
Feeds him his strength again in slow sharp drops,
And strength restores him to the outer room.

Keeping his eyes upon the watching face
He does not hope to alienate or fly,
He mentions gravely the inclement night,
Fetches a blanket for the couch. And then
The worst befalls—the face profoundly changes
To friendship sudden as love.

Mr. Tantripp's Day

I HE LIT THE STOVE ON A CLOUDY MORNING

The appalled heart at goosegray dawn,
As pale as ash, as old as lichen,
Goes down the stair in dogged flesh,
Beats coldly faint across the floor.
He takes both through the swinging door
Into the empty early kitchen.

The feather-sky sags on a mountain
Black-masked and eyeless as a mole—
He peers into the stove's round hole,
As chilly as a witch in hovel,
Then sends his diamond-hungry shovel
Into the swart slick shine of coal.

Now the heart kindles under its rib
For up, moon-size, the sun-disc goes
And burns the milky mist to blue
And purifies the dark to wonder.
He warms his hand where pulses under
The stove-lid purgatory's rose.

II HE BROUGHT THE MORNING PAPER FROM THE MAILBOX

Like lovers they move to this, like lovers in their trance,
Always toward each other; hot or cold,
Moon, neon, candle, sun; in every weather
That is not yet this weather,
Like lovers the killer and his to-be-killed
Choose, move, maneuver. Like lovers in a dance

Still strangers, ignorantly still, advancing they use
The lesser intimacies: summer, a smashed wave,
Spaghetti instead of clams; an evening of laughter;
Select the kind of laughter;
Are afraid, but not of this. Like lovers, like dancers, they move
By choice, but draw nearer with each motion they choose.

And always while they fumble for change, whistle, sleep
Under each other's moon, choose the polka-dot tie,
The canary sweater, the days like veils dissolve
Fast fast and faster; they descry
Naked and steep the ultimate intimate sight:

The animal struggle, if only in the eyes' pain,
In turn flashes—like dying warlock fought—
Through serpent, fox, dove; to the last pose
The held submissive pose
Of forever. The sudden Escaped, the towering Caught.
They came to this around childhood corners and adolescent rain.

III   AND AFTER DUSK THERE WAS A SHOW OF SLIDES

The three looked, across the room, straight on
The Spanish mountains
Big and wild and dark. Shone
Sunny haycocks; shone at their base
A field of wheat; acres of wheat
And vertical navy miles of mountain.

They breathed great air in that focused cheat
Of heavenly distance
When hairy darkness sat on wheat
Suddenly. A black and giant fly
Blotted the haycocks and the gold
And set his fly-legs across distance:

Four balanced his hugeness, he briskly whetted
Two; like a toy
Of fear he stopped their breaths, he netted
Their breaths in the evil gauze of his wings
Flung over yellow wheat and cocks
Of hay. Then he moved, like an ugly toy

And reason and faith ran. Down dropped
The stupid breath.
The fragile monster started, stopped,
Pittered over a tiny mile of boulders
And black suddenly into blackness went,
Releasing Spain and screen and breath.

IV   WITH THE ANCIENT DOG, HE STEPPED OUTSIDE
     AT MIDNIGHT

With him went the black small beast.
A dark wind shook the tamarisks
But could not blow the stars and moon about.

The dog had always vanished;
Never, once, come back unasked
Till now, tonight, quick as though menaced

By something in the humor
Of signals: the wind's tentative sound,
That watch-and-wait of eyes, stellar and lunar.

For close to the dog was a shape.
By the lit door love stood its ground.
The dog looked up in fear, in habit and hope.

At just this balance, beast and human,
The windy midnight spoke two words
Old and new for them to hear in common

Distinctly: *love* and *death*.
Then they moved, separate, and the door
Shut them inside together, for tonight at least.

And through the smallest hours
The still house like a brittle spar
Rode out the night among the jagged stars.

The Wind in the Sunporch

The chinese windchimes
stir
suddenly thin glass rings on thin glass
great leaves
nod
sideways sideways petals stir
to let it pass
clang-cling it plays.

My ribs lift up and
fall
my parted lips could dance a feather
under my palms both
your shoulder-blades fall and
lift
together with that huge light breath.

Poems for My Cousin

I took my cousin to Prettyboy Dam.
A boxer was swimming for sticks, the ripples
Blew from the left, and beer cans glittered
Under the poison-ivy.

We talked of pelota; and of how the tendrils of vines
Curl opposite ways in the opposite hemispheres.
My cousin was dying. By this I mean
The rate of his disengagement was rapid.

There was a haze of heat, and August boys
Chunked rocks at a bottle that bobbed on the water.
The slow hours enclosed the flight of instants,
Melted the picnic ice.

Everything he saw differently, and more clearly than I.
The joined dragon-flies, the solid foam of the fall;
The thin haste of the ant at my foot,
And me, as I looked at him.

We were close beside each other, speaking of
Pelota, chaining cigarettes when the matches were gone.
But we saw different things, since one could not say
"Wait . . ."
Nor the other "Come . . . "

II THE FOUR FACES OF MY COUSIN

My cousin had four faces.

One was the face which grimaced
In laughter or anger—mobile to danger,
Fun or sudden love;

Made up of flaws, joys, private
Recall; of a benediction
Or so, and sudden love;

With the harassed grain, and strains
Of wretched encounters, the thought
Of difficult heaven, and sudden love.

The second, was the blast of agony:
Contorted, it glared without sight
When the sheet was turned from the face

By familiar fingers. It glared
Without rest under the harsh gesture
Of death, and the mouth was frantic for its breath.

The third, silent, and silently watched
By the crucified man, had tiny pulses
Of light on its false tranquility—

The candle's mark. It was a good mask,
Composed to duty and not unbeautiful
Below the poised and frilly inner lid.

But the gray-white was wrong, and the faint rouge
On a dead man's lips—(and the fingers
Curled stiffly, shared the face's error).

The fourth face of my cousin I have never
Seen. This is the secret accurate intended
Face I must wait for.

III   ARRIVAL OF MY COUSIN

My cousin is arrived in
the green city of the dead.
It slopes, shapes itself
in hilly contours, and the summer light
lights all the white stones, crosses and angels of granite.

Thousands or tens of thousands
in the cool grass, under the flight
of birds, of shadows of birds; the shadow
of flight in the sunny marble,
the bird-notes, bird-calls, dew-clear;
The blue and white sky is bent over my cousin,
in the green city of the dead.

Traffic sweats and stalls on Oliver Street,
and Hargrove, Dolphin, Bethel Streets; the dirty bars
sweat, and the usual accidents in the accident-rooms
are glazed by July, as are the gutters and the junk-man's
horse, jerked up the tar-soft mountain of July.
My cousin, however, is in
the green city of the dead.

Not being of a primitive tribe
I speak in metaphor when I find my cousin,
cloud-free, granite-still, in
the green bird-rich city, bounded
by the sweating streets, and the houses, and rooms,
and the people in streets, houses, rooms,
and their eyes.
By the body of Christ we ate, his absence
is evident:
But I speak of the token, the image
I was given for identity;
that word of flesh, like a name, a sound,
is what I speak of.

Infinitely not of the alley, the gutter, the traffic,
the sweating problem that walks
the pavement, sits in the room—
is the token, the word, the vanishing image of my cousin
under blue sky, white cloud, grass, bird-call, stone angle
in the green city of the dead.

Time Exposure

Never can spring be known so well
As in this wicked dark December,
Nor touched—all emerald and limber—
As in this winter citadel.

The expatriate, in every country,
Encountering alien custom, presses
More closely to the land that graces
His memory, secret, beyond sentry;
The lover in the crowded room
Empty of the one essential,
Creates the missing face, more vital
More fresh than when it touched his own.
So now the death chill at the core
As if the weather struck with fangs,
So now the absence of all wings
Upon the harsh and scentless air,
Propose to the sick heart a stir
More subtle and a texture brighter
Than it has known or will encounter
In any earthly calendar;

The positive
Formed from this evil negative,
Shows what no year will ever give:
Spring's absolute.

Variations on a Theme

Harlequin speaks by the moon's light:
By the light of the moon, Peter, my friend
Peter, from your dark window bend

(Dark and moon and shadow blend)
To listen at least. (The bare boughs soar,
Pencil the wild white snow) lend

Me your cold gold pen to write
By the bright moon, Peter, my friend,
One word. One single word, no more.

The cold step of the hungry whore
Strikes on the stone, the cold stars bend
Over my small dead candle-end,

My naked hearth is dead tonight
I have no fire there to mend.
For God's love, open your door.

The Animal inside the Animal

*If an animal lives and moves, it can only be, he (the savage) thinks, be-
cause there is a little animal inside which moves it; if a man lives and
moves, it can only be because he has a little man or animal inside who
moves him. The animal inside the animal, the man inside the man, is the
soul . . .*

*. . . to this some of the blacks replied, Yes, yes. We also are two, we also
have a little body within the breast.*   THE GOLDEN BOUGH

I   THE ANIMAL INSIDE

The animal inside the animal
is motionless or moves. At midnight, paces.
Almost is ambushed in the mirror.

When his eyes open inward—not to see
but for your sight—its glimpsed shadow is beautiful, dangerous

only to this companion whose it is.
Seen, it can be loved. But how
it is terrible inside the breast.

Here it cannot be caught
to kill or free or tame.
It turns, and goes, and turns,

but rarely, at odd times.
Most often it is still;
as if asleep, or listening.

II SHADOW-NOTE

There is this footnote to the shadow:
It has the cruelty of innocence.
It will neither make excuses nor give details,
As: this is how it happened . . .
Or: how worn his face was . . .

So that the particular body throws
The universal shadow on the sand,
Carpet, pine-needles, cement, grave-sod—
Telling one thing: the truth
Without proportion, by its mass.

Where the substance would reach the doubtful senses,
The shadow goes past, immediate and in depth,
To your most private recognition
Of a gallows on gravel,
A cat on bright grass.

III SHADOW IMAGE

The short shadow
Squat and flat
Dwarfs the bole, says short is true;
The tall shadow
Says giant, giant.
But the tree lifts, says green on bluest.

On the black rainbow
Of wet sand
Flies over fast and tilted wing:
The gull's shadow.
And the hand
Casts on the dust its shadow-fingers.

The dark soul
Is shadow-word
Of the beast or man, the dark map
Of its soul, the shade of the bird
For which they set a shadow-trap.

IV   SHADOW WATER IMAGE

The houses waver in the water, waver,
flow over, stain and shudder.

Distorted, faithful, nothing is ignored,
all—contour, color—paired;

all—color, contour—changed. Untouchable:
water is brick and gable.

If the midnight heart, hunting love's face
meets in its place

his own, now will he drown, by such a loss,
in the silent brightness.

Narcissus, ravished, leaned a long moment
over this element:

the water-image then with a light shiver
drew down its lover

letting the fountain-laughter play its gleam
over the rooted bloom.

The Eyes of Children at the Brink of the Sea's Grasp

The eyes of children at the brink of the sea's
Grasp, dilate, fix; their water-sculpted hair
Models their heads; crouching a little they stare
In motionless ecstasy of panic
As the upreared load, tilting, tilting titanic
Pitches and shocks them in a rainbow crash
And is upon them in a cat's flash
Before the nearest shrieks and flees.
Most true terror carries them high to us
Up sand as white and dry as safety—thereafter
Gooseflesh and shudders rack them to drunken laughter,
They reel, self-conscious, pantomiming . . .
But presently sober, cautious down the shining
Dark slope of invitation, outward, to the prize
Of shaping danger they go—and widen their eyes
Innocent and voluptuous.

Tree Angel

Sang the angel in the tree:
pain prises the heart. See it stretch!
Narrow as the grave it was,
sang the leafy angel.

Fire in the marrow! sang
the angel in the tree,
pain pain on the inmost quick
another wave of it rises.

Pure pain taken
in the marrow the core the spirit's vein,
sang the birdy angel:
to your height it has added a cubit.

Suite for All Clowns' Day

CLOWNS' MARCH

Ladies! And likewise Gentlemen!
We are the clowns, we are the Clowns.
We were baptized with the mot juste—
Joey, and Charlie, and Auguste;
Our names are more than names—are nouns.
We are the clowns, your several Clowns.

Under the lights, and in the dark,
We are the clowns, we are the Clowns,
And we have learned that dogs do bark
Not only at beggars in the dark.
Our fingers gloved, our faces doughy,
Our titles Charlie, and Auguste, and Joey,
We are the clowns, your several Clowns.

Parade before you, cleansed of caution,
We are the clowns, we are the Clowns,
Alike your nightmare and your potion,
We are your trinity sans caution
Your loss and victory sans parley.
We, Joey, and Auguste, and Charlie,
In your small hearts, in your tall towns,
We are the clowns, your several Clowns!

CLOWNS' TURNS

I

Charlie never had any dignity, Charlie didn't.
His intention was starry but his luck was foul;
He tried very hard to save his soul,
But if dividend and divisor fetch the quotient,
Charlie was hopeless. His agape was strong,
But his inventory wasn't worth a song.
And Charlie never had any dignity, Charlie didn't.

Charlie tried to be brave, wanted to be clever,
He knew a lot and was on the right side,
But something uproarious happened to his pride,
He never triumphed, never, never, NEVER.
You could call him a hero fairly or a boob,
A citizen of the City of God or a terrible rube,
Certainly he wanted to be brave and tried to be clever.

Charlie wept tears, but Charlie was a comic.
He pickled the sick, the inept, the old, in brine,
But prat-falls and custards were in Charlie's line,
His gifts were funny rather than histrionic—
He tried for dignity, but dignity slipped him,
He tried for magnitude, but his big shoes tripped him.
Charlie wept tears, but Charlie was a comic.

II

As I swing from his tail the hooves of the galloping roan batter before
      my nose,
Then I must let go and roll in the sawdust shame and away he goes.
But a gleaming general told me, Joe, I haven't a man that brave.
The ringmaster willing, I could walk his tight-rope till doomsday's duck
      and after,
But I cheat my spine and the balls of my feet and I flail and I fall in the
      laughter.
But a judge in his robes said, Joey, you know more about rope than J.
      Ketch or a sailor.
In the brittle winter's waste with sweat and pride I shape my difficult
      game
And hotly I wait for the flowering spring, to pluck my public shame.
But a scarecrow saint in the ripe corn said, Brother, I am His patient
      clown.

III
Caesar and saint of court and canvas,
August Auguste, you come to try
The children crowded under canvas
You never meant to terrify.
Too thickly lashed the little eye.
The giant mouth is red. Mechanic,
Juggler, dog-walker, laugh or cry,
The undercurrent of their mirth is panic.

You are too old, Auguste, and show it,
It was not only Noah survived the flood.
You are too big and you should know it—
Your sawdust shadow shades the blood.
At midnight king's and hermit's mood
Heats from your small sad barbs that fester.
Your little dog is comic food,
Frankfurters for the giant deathless jester.

Isn't your circuit of the tent enough?
The child may find you in the meadow.
Your circuit of the tent is not enough.
White doppelgänger, cruciform and narrow,
You scatter by your clownish shadow
Our dubious pigeons
                              home to roost,
                                        august
                                            Auguste.

CLOWNS' SONGS

Sang Charlie, I cannot learn
If I am beautiful or not.
My glass has a crack.
He sang, The chestnuts burn
More hotly than I thought,
My blistered paw is black—
        Sang Charlie the clown.

Joey sang, My trapeze is flown
Like a bird and left me silly
And I slip, and flip
Down
      down
          down
Smack on my belly
In the net and up—
        Sang Joey the clown.

Sang Auguste, At midnight quite alone
Light the white light above the mirror;
My mask's big cliché—
The lips turned up or down—
(Is it the glass's error?)
Has nothing to say,
        Sang Auguste the clown.

Pitch Lake

The underworld was beneath the earth's surface, but above the nether waters, the great abyss.   Introduction to THE EPIC OF GILGAMESH

Erishkigal, Ishtar's fresh sister, sky-
goddess, darkened to a queen of shadows,
she too a shade.
She never came back, unlike Persephone
released to gilded meadows
on the flowers' tide.

There are two motions here: Persephone's
and the sister's. The first led up
to the place known
and the face. The second, to where dust lies
on door and bolt, and hope drops.
That motion led down.

Through the Trinidad blaze no gaze can be trusted:
the pontooned truck seems motionless to our eyes
as we step warily where
like a desert but blueback, heaved, crested,
now, here, the pitch lake lies
in noon's stare.

Actually it is sinking—but so smooth, so light,
so noiseless . . . the men who shine and bake
to load it know;
one will leap to loose the pitch grip at the right
last instant—the stirred stiff lake
will let it go.

But its skeleton sister was caught in the bubble
of black, in the shift of shiny suck.
Someone was late.
So the men did their best by expensive trouble;
knowing the law of gravity-in-luck,
they gutted the wraith.

It is half under, gradually grim.
But only insects or the smallest mice
go where it goes,
except for minnows that appear and swim
in tiny pools like fissures in black ice
that open. And then close.

At all costs, no symbols—one motion
is up. The other, down. This bright
black sets forth
what is familiar to passion or caution.
Fatally knowing, we step, lightly, to fixed earth.

They Never Were Found

The odd, the inward turned, the isolated:
The old gent who raises cats in his bedroom;
(A bright-eyed folk, quick through the doors
And made happy by fish);
Mr. Fleet who converses with his dead daughter
Over boiled milk on the kitchen range at midnight;
The elderly lady in the sailor hat
Who rides a scooter to the bank
From which she withdraws a little—only a very little.
She has a fat and shining balance in that bank
On the day when, the milk being accumulated,
Neighbors force the lock:
The air bad, no furniture, but three great piles of rubbish;
On the third the mistress of the house, quite dead by starving.

This was their fort-life, beleaguered, unallied—
One by his stove,
One on her scooter,
One in the dangerous company of his cats.

The Starfish

The great starfish was hauled up by a point.
Yellow and crimson with hard intricate bumps
it blazed wetly O it was regal and starry,
heavy cool cousin marine in the washy wave
a star a star.

But it was alive.

Its shape had a link with the steely stellar
steadfast light—no less than in ether
it conformed to its points of a star.

The sun strange as hot hell
attacked it in the grass. It could not
move. But it did. It
curled faintly

in the first sign of corruption—the distortion
of proportion,
of the correspondence between relative points. O a star
is not haphazard, only sickened
to death;
so, two points went
off center and the middle warped lightly.

It was a race.
Would the ants
clean it before irreparable corruption?
To gut a star
is a job—the ants were overtaxed.
There is a technique in destruction-through-preservation of starfish:

To pleasure the pink lady's project a
gentle black boy
placed it on an anthill.

The ants worked, worked, small, shiny, quick.
They came too late; the
water's stellar space in the wave's wash
     or
the coral bed had corresponded to the nothing neighborhood
of a star.

Like a tide the light of color drew back, tide, tide
sucked by the wicked wick of sun:
the shape went even more off starshape.

The connection snapped.
Even before the ants finished
it had disappeared from the categories of desire

its silent cool marine starlife warm and warped
its starhood stung to chaos.

Here is your sting. O
death, where is your star?

Yellow

Yellow became alive.
Materialization took place.
First logically with lemons,
then fresh butter.
Also a chairleg.
After that it appeared
to carve the curve of clouds
and, as sun, shatter them.
The stars grew yellower
yellow whirls on wheels on whirls
leaves flew yellow
the corn sprang
yellow and the crows
winged with a yellow nimbus.
Finally his face
had brilliant yellow
in its grain.
Outside the madhouse hung the yellow sun.

Country Bath

He was naked in water,
the house all quiet, the raw bulb hanging,
when the great June bug
came booming and crashing
thutter and thutter and soft pop deadly
against the raw brilliance.

Outside the night stared like a monster
million-eyed, gold-eyed, over the mountains;
not a clock-tick, a tap-drip, just
that stutter and thunder.

Then hurt and thrashing and lying and dying
and silence. So he saw
what had only been known; all alone, and at night:
how light

burns.

The Enemy of the Herds, the Lion

The enemy of the herds, the lion, feeds on its prey on decorated box-lid,
ca. 2500 B.C., which was found in the grave of the Lady Shub-ad
at Ur.   NATURAL HISTORY MAGAZINE

At Ur
the lady Shub-ad's small
bright box went into the larger darker
shelter of the grave and stayed there roughly
forty-five hundred years.

Its lid—
a sharp arc—shows a thing:
a lion-sheep without division,
lion on top, sheep under, still
consummation point.

The sheep
neck is in the lion fangs
the lion claws press upward the sheep throat, they are
tranced and ardent in act of taking
utter enough to be love.

Back so far
the mind tires on the trip:
so close, the salve or kohl to redden
the lip, lengthen the eye for pleasure's
pleasure, is tonight's.

What is changed?
Not the coarse hairs
of the mane; victor, or victim; a woman's body;
certainly not a death; not the colors
of kohl or scarlet.

She
cared for the box; by wish
expressed or guessed she took it along
as far as might be. Why this one? What
word did her box-beasts mean?

Possi-
bilities; the chic symbols
of the day, on a fashionable jewel-toy,
the owner modishly ignorant; or, corrupt,
an added pulse to lust.

Or:
mocking, or wise, remembrance
of innocent murder innocent death,
the coupled ambiguous desire,
at dinner, at dressing, at music.

Or,
best, and why not? of her meeting
all quiet terror, surmounted by joy,
to go to her grave with her; a pure
mastery older than Ur.

Deaf-Mutes at the Ballgame

In the hot sun and dazzle of grass
The wind of noise is men's voices:

A torrent of tone, a simmer of roar,
And bats crack, bags break, flags follow themselves.

The hawkers sweat and gleam in the wind of noise,
The tools of ignorance crouch and give the sign.

The deaf-mutes sit in the hurricane's eye,
The shell-shape ear and the useless tongue

Present, but the frantic fingers' pounce-and-bite
Is sound received and uttered.

If they blink their lids—then the whole gaudy circle
With its green heart and ritual figures

Is suddenly not: leaving two animal-quick
Wince-eyed things alone; with masses and masses

And masses of rows of seats of men
Who move their lips and listen.

While secret secret sits inside
Each, his deaf-mute, fingerless.

Painter at Xyochtl

He had a devil's look; and no rain—
The Mexican jungle rain-hungry,
The gods certainly angry,
The Mexican earth in dry pain—
The birds thirsty and the men and the grain.

But even with his mysterious coming, and his skin,
And the drought's brassy eye
The chief said, "Let him say.
If he is not a devil, let him begin—"
(Though he has come, and with the color of sin.)

In the dialect he could not say "Yes" or "No," "Old" or "Young."
But the chiefs waited, even then,
While a runner fetched the men
(Two) who could speak the Outside tongue.
They were reasonable and patient, though the drought had been long.

It was Spanish, of course. He could only plead
In English, in German. He cried, not in the Inside
Nor the Outside tongue, in his public need
He gibbered hell's speech.
But a devil can bleed.

Quartered, they carried him, within the rite,
North, South, East, West. The rains
Came promptly to the grains'
The men's, the birds' dry throats.
And flowers sprang like speech, to sight.

Note: A few years ago, a young German-American painter was the victim of a ritual murder at the hands of some remote Central American Indians into whose village he strayed alone during a prolonged drought.

Landscape Finally with Human Figure

The sky stainless, flawed by one gull
And stretched across no sight, silk-tight;
salt noon stranded like a hull
in clearest light;

clarity of palms splits the sun
to strike and shiver on the blue blue view,
so perfection not ended nor begun
is perfectly true.

The hollow setting (while the jewel lags),
infinite, unsoiled, smiling, clear:
            Appear!
Sly, dirty, cruel, lost and in rags
the beloved is here.

49th & 5th, December 13

I passed between the bell and the glass
window. Santa rang his bell. The wax girl leaned
forward: she was naked and had red nails.
Santa wore spectacles and rang his bell.
The second-floor trees raised rainbows in the dusk.

The snow fell lightly. I did not stop to ask
the scarlet man a favor; the girl leaned as if to give
from her wax body blood or heat or love.
But she was wax. Her belly and breasts were shaped;
she wore black pumps and leaned, above the pavement.

The unique snowflake died on the cement.
I passed between her wax eyes and his clapper.
The steelrimmed eyes watched me, the wax eyes watched the watcher.
He rang, she leaned, to give me my message: that I must breed
alive unique love from her wax and his steel.

Arrival of Rain

At midnight
it began to rain.

The sound of rain everywhere
fills my hollow ear.
The dry weeks round I was not thinking of that sound—
two sounds, the sound
of falling and the sound of drinking—
now here.

Dusty root darkens and the stubble sharpening
its cruel shafts, softens;
my hollow ear harkening
hears stubble green and moisten,
all drinking, all darkening;
the liquid beaded sigh
of sound, two sounds
everywhere and here
in the hollow avid ear.

All need is dry.
Rain is the metaphor.

The Uninvited

Like dew the children beckon to the dry,
Like heat they shimmer to the winter eye;
Limpid and lovely, comfort is their presage:
The glass wall clearly mirrors us, who try
The foolish, hopeful, undeliverable message.

We are not bidden to the birthday meal—
We are distinct from these by blood and steel.
Our tenderest vines have known nocturnal foxes,
The clock's thin hands have crucified our zeal
And we have nailed our dead in wooden boxes.

Mourner Betrayed

He trusted death when it said "I am the end!
Nothing exists now!" But the truth
Seemed that the creeping June-green growth
Covers the face of death and does not mind.

The sun is savage, the grass powerful—
The orchard scents and shadows filter
Into his mind where death sought shelter . . .
He gives it, in his harried heart, a lull.

"Death!" says the heart, grim as a hard-pressed fencer,
"Death, the implacable, death the forever!"
But the white May-clouds in stillness travel over
And the fierce dandelions do not answer.

April Asylum

The mad old women, bolted from April's weather,
Sit, in their morning rows, cautious, intent,
And Technicolor, like a sacrament,
Is raised to bless the lonely and together.

In the barred window ten o'clock puts free
Gilt on the potted lily; air outside
Stirs up to scent the petalled plum-tree's tide
Boiling surf-white on the blue ether-sea.

Sheltered by iron, washed and dressed and fed,
Resistant to motion foreign as a wing—
Before it moves the sea, behind it, spring,
This audience of docile sentient dead.

Repeating white on blue, the seascape screen
Crests, crashes, curdles; on this dim locked beach
Neat sit the mad old women (cautious, each
Gray secret face raised quietly) between.

The Lion-house, the Elephant-house, the Snakes, were Sunday wonder,
And "Zoo," echoes the mind; but the childish fear was fun,
And now along the adult horizon ruffles the muffled thunder.

The rain holds off. In simple dark equality of plight
The similarities, though superficial, run:
(Peanuts subtracted, shirt-sleeves and drinking-fountains and delight),

Hygiene; slant, sun-made bars across cement; the sound of keys
On ring; the terminology: Identity, Adult Female,
Although at feeding-time the kindly keeper calls "Louise!"

But where the lynx lay watchful on its gray fake treestub
And the hippo blew and floated monstrous in its stale
Small pool and up the piled rocks toiled the frowsy bear-cub

Lay jungle isolation like a blessing. And never never
The thread that leads to distant nerves in tangled fever
Of thin tough pain, that leads to loves no rational knife can sever.

III   THE STORM CLEARED RAPIDLY

Over the dripping fruit-trees breaks the sky
Plum-blue to angel-blue,
The bird-calls shimmer, glittering-new
Curls for the visitor the gravel drive

Where, on the blazing grass, sits the wet granite,
Abadon's solid shelter,
The structure season shall not alter,
Housing the private and disastrous climate.

IV   WHEN THE PATIENT PASSED BY THE MUSIC TEACHER
     WAS PRACTICING IN THE OPEN WINDOW

The weeping crabapple trails its pink tradition,
The plum shakes thickly white because of seed,
The algebra of grass recites its creed:
Green + soft × silent furious fission
= this breed.

The flute-notes fall contemplative and single,
Linked in a chain of never-more-nor-less,
Over the architectural happiness
The tufted titmouse, under the sun-hot shingle,
Constructed with success.

Above move clouds in current, underneath
Flow capable earthworms, functional and mute;
Black bloom on white and gala as a wreath
The notes in logic cluster: human breath
Counts clearly on the flute.

Only, on the purposeful path, obscene and frail,
Weaves weak from edge to edge the menaced stranger,
Opposing the cherry, the plum; the loose-mouthed Male,
Carrying as usual the empty and purposeless pail.
Alone, in danger.

Errant beneath the normal blossoms' force,
Under the fragrance from their thousand throats,
Flanked by green blades, unarmed, without a course
Alone alone where fall without remorse
The deadly notes.

The Birds

Corrigan knew that loneliness is the one human passion;
"The bird-voices cry," he said, "each in its ego's tone,
But the theme is the same," he told me, "whatever the musical fashion:
The cry of a half a thing, divided, and so, alone."

He told me their notes: Vanity cries "I am beautiful, therefore love me!
I am Rose, Blue, Green! Love me!" thin and high;
And Fear cries, deep from the swamp, "No, no, you do not love me!
You will injure me!" Corrigan said in the night you can hear it cry.

"I am severed," cries Passion, "Love me! Unite me! See, I am severed!"
Crazily crying in the spruces over the unlistening snow,
"See, I am severed! Love me! Unite me!" crazily fevered,
Over and over, Corrigan said, till the cocks crow.

From the maple at noon Wealth cries "Love me, for I am rich! Hear!
        Hear my sum!"
(Wealth crying forlornly, "Love me!" under the August heat),
And Power, "Love me, for I can hurt you!" with the sky like a plum,
And the storm in the oaks, "Love me, for I can hurt you!" he heard it
        repeat.

And over the orchard-grass, from the apple, the apple crusted with
        bloom,
At dawn the lover cries in the mixed and melting dark,
"Love me, for I love you," in the early green gold gloom,
Crying ". . . for I love you! Love me!" from the dewy bark.

"And from the wood ahead, from the forest behind, in all weathers,
And always," said Corrigan, "always by blackness and sun, from the
        wood, ahead,
The soul, crying to God, 'Love me!' from the thin desperate shelter of
        feathers,
'Love me! Love me forever, for I must live!'" Corrigan said.

PART THREE

1965

1970

Reindeer and Engine

The reindeer
fastened to the great round eye
that glares along the
Finnish forest track
runs runs runs runs runs
before that blast of light, will die
but not look back

will not
look back, or aside, or swerve
into the black tall deep
good dark of the forests of winter
runs runs runs runs runs
from that light that thrust through his brain's nerve
its whitehot splinter.

The reindeer
has all the forests of Finland to flee
into, its snowy crows and owlly
hush; but over the icy ties
runs runs runs runs runs
from his white round i-
dée fixe until he dies.

To his west
is wide-as-the-moon, to his right
is deep-as-the-dark, but
lockt to his roaring light
runs runs runs runs runs
the fleeing flagging reindeer
from, into, the cold
                    wheels'
                         night.

Colloquy

"Why? Tell me why?" he said in dismay to Corrigan,
"Should happiness, golden happiness, the profound, the acute,
Be speechless, be dumb; be the song, be the poem of no man,
Silent as the little mermaid, as the broken nightingale, as all the mute?

"Out of the dark of centuries the accents of sorrow break,
From antiquity full and generous, without stint or ration:
From the loss of love, from the waste spaces, from the candescent stake,
Comes articulate music—the word's memorable passion.

"I will have speech for my happiness," he said doggedly, "speech that is
     fit
Now while it is full of strength, while it is fierce and young!"
"And did you think," said Corrigan, "that the Watchers had not spoken
     for it?
Did you think the Watchers of happiness had not given it tongue?

"Are the deep voices pitched too low for your ear, under the rain
Lashing the shelter, the low voices under the howling weather?
Death patiently saying, 'If I must wait, I must wait,' and pain
Saying to loneliness, 'Tonight they will sleep together.'"

The Minor Poet

The minor poet sits at meat
with danger smoldering in his eye,
to left, to right, his dicta fly,
impaling those who blot or botch:
should any dolt essay reply
his voice goes up another notch.

Attempts to qualify are doomed.
Who could object? Which would displease?
With finger raised, in tones that freeze
he checks his points: 1, 2, 3, 4.
By salad time, the very cheese
is paler, for his scorn and lore.

Wit dies before his massy frown—
until, bethinking, from his files
he fetches forth a *mot,* and smiles!
And not a man or woman weeps,
though each one knows that we have miles
and miles to go before he sleeps.

The Greek Wind

This wind blows still in stone; blows
in still stone: this
stonestill wind lifts

the draped folds, rocks
the wing-tip, combs
back the stonecold curls.

The body breasts it, blown
almost back: the breasts are shaped
by the wind's touch: the breasts' breath

drinks it salt and fresh; in
the instant of centuries that salt
seawind bright

with invisibility, blows back
the fluent tender folds: watch
it tense the instep,

rush the neck's thrust. See:
it plows the stone like fluid wheat
in its passage.

The Coming

All day the children await the coming.
It is no good telling them that the hour is wrong,
that roses and bells must fall and the gate
wait, and the bees hush and a star
show itself, before the arrival.

It does not matter, much, whom
they await—someone beloved
coming with love and the refusal of a
request, and a disappointing present;
or a stranger, met, or heard about, or not.

What they attend never yet has come. Strange children
to wait so fiercely? Yet elders, in the city,
waiting the known guest as the clock bats out
softly the hour, and a rumor of voices—or is it
steps on the stair?—comes up, feel the heartbeat
falter: what sort of powerful presence
breathes, outside the thin door?

Daughter to Archeologist

Dear Father:
  You were a doctor. Perhaps your avocation,
sketchy and subterranean,
was concerned with curing, too.
We breathe through our future.
Remember me is the message. The rest
could be error, and very likely is.

The buried ship, the hound's skeleton,
the heavy-handled looking-glass
that took a face and lost it,
these and Mnemosyne, goddess of our tribe,
bless you. As I do. You, angel
of the chipped token,
the token resurrection.

A child,
I thought of Egypt as a giant tomb
full of blind brilliance buried and sealed.
I see a scarab you wore, on my finger.

The owners of gold, cloth, breastbone, are part of silence,
until like a bell, light strikes.
Then, *in memory of me* . . . says each.

Down you went to search them out.
Be remembered.

There Is Good News

a law
removing from use the monosyllable *love*
for a period of three years; pro-
mulgated by a poet, and un-
enforceable. But a law.

The monosyllable
(which I may no longer name)
will be unavailable to:
carbonated drinks; pimps; all ad-
vertising agencies; candidates;
graduation addresses;
haute couture; hill-billy
bands; and, under the worst penalties, all
Interested Parties.

This will deprive
children; those dying; lovers; and those
other needy. But it is hoped
that in the fourth year
someone as yet unknown
will enunciate a syllable
of force
so tall as to unite
roots and
heavenly bodies.

At Night

the eye closes:
that retina, three inches for the earth
    and the sky
        shuts its camera eye:
that day
    prepares to die,
be judged—be balanced and even,
    hungry and odd;
be purgatory, be
      débris of heaven.

What small
    metaphors we set
ourselves: the three-inch flinching
      eye, the three-inch tyrant
heart, that took the day and all
adventures in. Or
the heart quailing and the savage
      eye: they can feel
    the wind, the heart hear
sounds: now, small instruments, hush:
    beat softly, heart, shutter yourself,
      eye:
contract and tell your size
    in sleep. Sizes are games. What
      size is just
    to hold
God's windy light,
    the small dry tick of hell?

The Primer

I said in my youth
"they lie to children"
but it is not so.
Mother my goose I know
told me the truth.

I remember that treetop minute.
That was a baby is a woman now;
in a rough wind, it was a broken bough
brought down the cradle with the baby in it.

I had a dumpy friend (you would not know his name,
though he indeed had several), after his fall
lay in live pieces by my garden wall
in a vain tide of epaulets and manes.

I had another friend (and you would know her name),
took up her candle on her way to bed.
She had a steady hand and a yellow head
up the tall stairwell, but the chopper came.

So small they meant to run away, from sightless eyes
three mice ran toward my mind instead;
I seized the shapely knife. They fled
in scarlet haste, the blind and tailless mice.

Cock robin was three birds of a single feather.
Three times cock robin fell when a breeze blew;
eye of fly watched; arrow of sparrow flew:
three times cock robin died in the same weather.

Sheep, cows, meander in the corn and meadow;
soundless the horn, fine, fine my seam;
nothing I feed, but rosy grows my cream.
My blue boy sleeps under the stack's huge shadow.

Notes from a Lenten Bar

I know that my redeemer liveth because
the pebble-eyed gent with the briefcase
two tables down has called him by name
3 times in 2 and ¾ minutes;
and because
the guys on my right are liquid with the health
of victorious Immaculate Conception, 46 to 98;
and because
after the last of my supper, I learn once more
as I rise to 1403
there is nothing between the 12th and the 14th floor.

Insomniac's Bird

The first clear faint unlocated call
through the whole dark reaches the ear.
At that, the gothic shapes of guilt and doom break stride;
the hard obsessive patter of the detail
hot on the naked heel, the hours' coil,
the pulsing pause that is neither there, nor here,

collapse. Light will define the fringes of the fern;
the bird will bring it and the grass will deepen it.
O the good stir and rumor. You can go
now into its promise, as the dark tide turns,
stranding the hulk of apple trees and barn,
floating stars westward. Therefore, waker, sleep.

Waker, though the soaked fields lie without a sound,
since that single note, feel how the dark is crazed
like a plate; and what far fire did that, will come
to show green, grown out of the sightless ground,
wings trust air, and fingers form their hand.
Now is the act of sleep quick, true and easy.

Bush

It is the sound of lions lapping.
They drink themselves
from the gold shapes that waver
and grow shallower.

Blue peels itself in the waterhole; it is the sun coming.
Crouched, the lions meet
their matches at the surface.

The foxy jackals are far off
but the vultures cloud the flat treetop;
the drum of the zebra's body
is lined with red sunrise.

The jackals and vultures are waiting
for what happened under the moon.
The lions are through with it; they
lift their dripping chins and look ahead.

It is six o'clock on Christmas morning.
Now the lions have stopped lapping
the bush makes no sound
the vultures shift, but without sound.

The day is perfectly seamless.
Slowly the lions move like pistons past the dry grasses;
the jackals do not move yet;
the vultures show patience.

The lions pass a thornbush and melt.
Though the whole day is unbroken
the passage of the sun will represent heaven;
the bones will represent time.

On My Island

they kill mongooses. Always, before they club
the trapped head, a formal greeting is offered:
"Good morning, Mr. Mongoose."
If they struck in silence, a sharp-toothed shade
would come for them: feral, affronted
to have been anonymous, unidentified,
unsaluted. After good morning and the courteous
title, if not the beast, his spirit, is appeased.

A man as murderer explained his situation's
anonymity: They didn't say, man, he said,
or woman, or child: he said, they just said
dead mongooses—no, communists. They didn't
say anything about age, or anything. So he never
thought to say, Good morning,
child.

Arrival

Up the path, past the iced birdbath and the black roses;
the street black, too. But the lamp at the door
shows the face: forbidden, totally forbidden.
Over the threshold. And downstairs the door unmistakably closes.

The only forbidden face, actually, truly forbidden: bare,
narrow and intent, colder than the yard's clay.
His intentions are intimate, no question of that.
He is not, in point of fact, hurrying, but has reached the turn in the
        stair.

Perhaps a brief visit? The disastrous and not-necessarily-fatal feet
are here and a knob turns. A sandwich perhaps, in a cardboard box?
A shared midnight snack? A thick suitcase in either hand?
Or is there a van, huge in the invisible street?

The Interrupted

Of the goddess there is only the marble shoulder and one
keen breast, lifted in a shout or love.
The axle is all that remains of the race.

On the smashed frieze, the forelegs, jubilant,
spring from no stallion: spring in the glass case
under the shadow of outside almond bloom.

On a stump, leafless, the slender headless youth
leans on his elbow, tenderly in stone,
to watch something in absence.

Acanthus cannot shake, though wind from the sea comes in:
the acanthus is a scrap from a scrap of column.
It is stopped short and waits for us.

The noble plunge of the stallion, the race, the shout,
the eyes' view, the acanthus moved by the wind
achieve themselves in this stone room—

of the company of their unbroken peers, the lords.
These escape from their maker's limit to rejoice us
with hope. These are the interrupted.

The Matadors

The dirty money and the sleazy hearts
swell the *fiesta brava;*
in cheap *sol,* dear *sombra,* sit the greedy
strong-armed with expendable cokes and cushions-
missile-rebukes of buyers to the bought:

pig-eyed, big-assed, the princes of peseta,
tycoon of horses, tycoon of *billetes,*
knowers of the greasy ropes, the skid;
aficionados of the tide that turns:

the bloodshock of the trumpets,
the celestial suit, the very sand
under the sole of the slipper
crying, what is sold a man
if he lose his profit?

Yet it is silly to say
that their blood and their wrists have not spoken,
the fighters with names like lights:
El Espartaro, Manolete, Josalito.
They speak to us.

The bulls were always there;
in the moonlit pastures,
moving through shadows
the blacker shadows.

They speak,
the matadors. To us.
Right-thinking cannot hush
them, nor the crowds, their enemy;
nor the gentle wish.

They will speak and we will answer.
Unless someone is born
who has not set himself
before the dark horned shape

alone,
set his feet in sand
calling softly, hoarsely,
Toro, toro! Venga!

My Small Aunt

      died in a dust of lions; her Africa
was secret as her body and arrived
like the biblical robber by night, by darkest night;
that night, however, was the cinema's:
where there before her, high and bright, and wide
as love, it stretched its radiant sinister light.
And by the foreground clump of pampas grass
shone the pride.

She knew it all before she saw it all.
Light-hearted as a warrior come home
she absolved its horrors: the bald-neck buzzards,
carrion-content; and in the waterhole
the gross great pigs that float their eyes on scum;
the cough, the red snatched meal, the hot-breathed hazard;
in what sense the pride goeth before the fall—
the hunted one.

Was she the hunter or the hunted? Both.
At home, the click and tick of cup and clock
failed to falter in any changes. Hunted
by pain, and tireless hunter of the moth,
she turned no key within a useless lock.
No nephew, nay, no friend, went disappointed.
But in her sun slept lions, chockablock
with blood and sloth.

She queued for her ticket in the stale winter street,
and, step for step, the mean wind cried like a ghoul
in her ear and flourished its trash and her blue eye wept.
But closer and close, the aromatic heat
and the flat trees; and like a homing soul
she met the spaces the hot grasses kept
and met the motion of four soundless feet:
the paced prowl.

Hunted or hunter. Too brave to be sad,
the fear of pity fixed her like a stare.
Sharp starry hunters, luminous orions
whirled in her sleep. Taking her cup in bed
she drank unsweetened courage black and clear.
In their gold ruffs waited the shining lions,
violent and sunny lords who never had
pity or fear.

"The Moon Will Restore the Virginity of My Sister"

CAMINO REAL

Over my paws
the violet lids are lowered, the varnished wasp's nest
bowed; the dial on her pulse flays her away
to tininess; the manicure is half over, the day
is half over, her life.

The silver talons flash on the small hard fingers.
No ring on the left hand, on the right
a ring the size of a mouse;
at the eyes' corners, over the lovely bones,
the reassembled waitings have put prints.

The channel of her hope curves back
very far. Chanel says she is a flower, as the silver nails
say she is lunar. O prepared, prepared
for the waited stranger's desire
encouraged this dark day early in the hostile glass.

She flips her towel and rolls her rosy vial
warming in palms her sacred senseless hope.
Over my nails' half-moons, bent like Picasso,
with catquick licks she paints my forty fingers.

The Lovers

The lovers lie in the shelter of night, the lovers
lie in each other's arms in night's crux:
the clock stopped and stars still and fire
unlit, in each other's arms lie the lovers.

Still clock and stopped stars are not true:
cold dust blows from the stars, cold iron roars
through space, time ticks trapped in the two
lovers' wrists. False, stopped clock and still stars.

On the cold hearth, to kindle the lovers' fire,
stuffed under logs lie inky rage and retribution;
on a nail on the wall, stretched arms and folded feet
hang and motionlessly reproduce an execution.

Here the stars make no sound, there is no wind, no clock.
Once an animal cried out in the tall cold meadow
grass, beyond the glass cried out, addressing owl or fox.
Who will stay the lovers in their single shadow?

The lovers lie in the shelter of their deaths;
though they move, now, to part, it is a feint at most:
who were two have died, and are safe in a single breath:
they are discovered, found with all the lost.

In the Crevice of Time

For Elliott Coleman

The bison, or tiger, or whatever beast
hunting or hunted, and the twiggy hunter
with legs and spear, in the still caves of Spain
wore out the million rains of summer
and the mean mists of winter:
the frightening motion of the hunter-priest

who straight in the instant between blood and breath
saw frozen there not shank or horn or hide
but an arrangement of these by him, and he himself
there with them, watched by himself inside
the terrible functionless whole
in an offering strange as some new kind of death.

The thick gross early form that made a grave
said in one gesture, "neither bird nor leaf."
The news no animal need bear was out:
the knowledge of death, and time the wicked thief,
and the prompt monster of foreseeable grief:
it was the tentative gesture that he gave.

Our hulking confrère scraping the wall,
piling the dust over the motionless face:
in the abyss of time how he is close,
his art an act of faith, his grave
an act of art: for all,
for all, a celebration and a burial.

The Class

The small black blobs on the beach are the heads
of children. Defectives:
the imbeciles could not come, and the morons
have graduated to lives.
Five sit under the sun at the tide's edge.

Everything moves: like a motion of silence a sailboat
goes on the sea's brilliant shiver;
the glittery palms make the sound of raining,
clouds change shape, waves curl over.
The five stay still as five struck in one pose.

They are out for an outing in the free great air:
they face the Caribbean;
the air will not bear them up, nor the sea,
nor the sand grow an herb to heal,
nor the thick white clouds transport them elsewhere.

This is no lesson the voice gives.
They listen, listen in a secret school,
their faces lifted: conscienceless, on their skin
the tongue of the tide says, *Cool* . . .
and in glazed brightness the sun says, *Live* . . .

The Mexican Peacock

For Flannery O'Connor

He presses the eight o'clock dew with short sharp paces,
the tail, laid plume on plume, balanced over the grass
by inches, dipping not touching; the stiff elegant
crest over the head level in motion as a queen's chin,
the ordinary toes carrying cautiously every ocellate
moon, sun, whorl, enjambment of color.

The waterlily cups have unclenched to the light:
white and pink still chilly, ixora and oleander,
moist still: but the Mexican sun is stoked and ready.
The peacock mixes blues and greens, deepens them, pauses,
preparing to celebrate himself in an invisible glass
that kindles a blue royal enough for a *pavo real.*

You, a woman not dazzling, and cripplingly caught,
moved as swift and pitiless as light, neither less nor more,
among the pinchbeck vanities, the mingy shifts
of the heart, the small shabby panics of the killer,
the lethal state of grace abrupt as a pitfall.
Intellect, intellect, love and shame occupied your power.

Yet the stupid, vain, ill-tempered peacock obsessed your desire
from child to death: the unfurled arc,
the eye of glory, the tilted head of a bad bird,
went straight to the center spot, the bullseye of mystery:
its maker's pleasure in a living thing
lovely and loveless as a pausing peacock

who pauses now, suddenly to hoist his soundless plumes
trembling and blazing in a fringy arc:
to the right he bows his crest; shudders his moons;
ignited by the sun, bows to the left.
That message of gratuitous pleasure, to the beholder,
in communion with our joy transfixed you.

Birdsong of the Lesser Poet

Exuding someone's Scotch in a moving mist,
abstracted as he broods upon that grant,
he has an intimate word for those who might assist;
for a bad review, a memory to shame the elephant.

Who would unearth a mine, and fail to work it?
His erstwhile hosts are good for fun and games
that brighten the lumpen-audience on the poetry circuit.
He drops only the most unbreakable names.

Disguised as youth, he can assign all guilt:
his clothes proclaim a sort of permanent stasis.
With a hawk's eye for signs of professional wilt,
he weeds his garden of friends on a monthly basis.

And yet, and yet, to that unattractive head,
and yet, and yet, to that careful, cagey face,
comes now and again the true terrible word;
unearned, the brief visa into some state of grace.

Treaty

See us, strangers from the land of embarrassed death,
where it is assumed everyone is always alive
and that the living are more numerous than the dead
who are only a few familiar names: Guatemala!
where everything belongs to the dead. They lend
a lodging in the World under strict laws;
from the tiny huddle the living cautiously closes
the old bargain, paying candles, copal and roses.

Paying roses, incense and candles to the ancestors,
to the owners of the World, a section of which he borrows,
to the watchers and guardians, the Lord of Crevices.
Payment for lodging, World, is 9 wax tapers,
½ pound of incense, 25 pesos of aguardiente,
5 ounces of sugar and 100 cakes of copal:
Hail World, and your owners, Masters of the Knives,
Masters of Rules, here is payment to all dead
Master Masons, Master Builders, Masters of Lead.

The flutes for the house, the flutes all night for dancing,
wandering, chaining, thin and pure, play in the shadow
of that attentive hosting; under their eyes perform
the marimberos and the tamboreros
faint in the hills until the cock calls light;
the corn climbs the barranco at their aegis
and their powerful bird, the purifying vulture,
black in the blue, down over the flowers' flame
drops his great shade, silent, in their name.

We can see this. Not even children, playing,
clean children, unobservant and important,
can miss the risky tenure of the house,
can impudently disbelieve the presence:
mountains, barrancos, flutes, marimbas, drums
address the multitude whose eyes we bear.
But now at dusk do not insist on our knowledge.
We are quick shadows, but strangers; who need, when all is said,
a private love, the English language, and a bed.

The Emperor's Cook

Laguipière, the Emperor's cook,
gastronomy's artificer and chart,
died in the retreat from Moscow,
having in view to the last the two
great themes of nourishment and art.

Ice-ribbed, the scarecrow dead;
a white vibration meant day.
His feasts froze in his brain.
Once he dreamed of his pupil, Carême;
he thought often of his peer, Bouché.

To the bony end, he thought of high
cuisine, august, enticing.
Finally, the glittering slick world
shone like a wicked cake's
megalomaniac icing.

It was like a bitter, short command,
not of word, or rouble,
but of posthumous honor coveted,
to serve the whole brilliant chef d'oeuvre
for some terrible table.

The Wild Parrots of Bloody Bay

Up from Bloody Bay are the hills
where the wild parrots live.
In pairs they fly
high and dark with harsh faint cries.

In the last sunlight the hurricane-
stripped trees point up up
to where in that thin soft gold air
they wheel and fly fast and together away.

But they descend too: on a distant bare tree
like Chinese ornaments,
without motion or pity
they sit burning in their own green:

then soundless up and off, careening
over the crests. To mock and to redeem
the obscene cracker and the puppet syllable
come the faint wild harsh screams.

The Foreign Lands

I saw a mongoose this morning ripple down the scarp,
hot blood over cold dew, about his savage trades;
up up over the crater lake, from where they screamed and flew
in pairs, the wild parrots drop down out of the upper air
to settle on blasted boughs and wait out dark.

Lizards live in my tree; puff out their throats
in a passion of silence, grow bold second tails under my very eyes;
insect-still, against the sky wait in a profile so old
it stirs my hair. Last night, by the steps, at my bare
foot, made out of tough cool dusk a toad was crouched.

Born travelers must and will have terra incognita:
wharf, port, the treecrest trace, fog's rumor of a coast.
But that escaping ghost, the genius of the place,
strangeness, moves its kin outward as the keel comes in.
Poor traveler, helplessly at home in Zanzibar, in Tierra del Fuego.

Timid or brazen, humble, acquisitive
traveler, this territory will not pall:
toad, parrot, the alien small, feathered, webbed, furry;
lizard, mongoose and bat, they loom like lands,
swing like stars, I watch; and wish to, may not, inherit.

The Chanterelles

Near the eighth tee, sixty yards off into the woods from the green links,
out of the dark spongy soil, yellow as finches or butter
the chanterelles grew suddenly by the black wet trunks
of firs in the sopping glade, where it was always later.

We were going home to cook our feast in cream and Neufchâtel
and onions, to devour it together close to the first flames
smelling of resin. Other mushrooms grew with the chanterelles,
some single, breastbone white; others the color of dust, the color of rain.

A furious chipmunk dug where something was buried
and prized; a big bird, pumping, blundered over us, once.
Food and fire and love waited. At the end, we hurried
our damp fingers. We had enough, perhaps in every sense.

In the needles' thick silence the air smelled of thunder,
our hands were cold on the fluty underpart;
when we straightened our backs, the pale mushrooms were paler.
As we came out on the links nothing moved behind us except the dark.

The chanterelles were royal; food and summers we ate;
yet, in their equinoxial flavor, understood
we dealt as well with cousins-german; with the shapes
of different mushrooms, near the links, in the mock-up wood.

Night Patrol

The wolf's cousin,
gentled to clown for us,
paces now, forbidden
to be trusted, or trust:
paces the pavement.

The black shoes and the furry toes
pace together on the wide
night street; from the raw light, pace
into the jungle shadows.
The wolf blood courses under hide.
The feet echo; silent go the paws.

A clock strikes winter.
Hunters are cold as hunted.
The dog teaches the man to listen:
something waits in the shadows' center.
The wolf heart knows what is wanted,
called back from a dream unnatural and human.

They walked like mutant friends, in a season's sun;
now they walk like wolves, and know their own.
Their own move toward them: empty, the street
moves toward them, where in this bitter season
cold wolf and wolf meet.

An Absence of Slaves

The Greek guide
said:
"I want you to remember one thing."
With her deep voice and curly
hair
and small shocked shoes, she said,
"This is our pride:

this was free
labor:
free men built this Par-
thenon. Athenians
left fold and press and field
and harbor:
gave no slavery."

The sun broke
on glorious stone, ripped from the dark
quarry; she said: "The city
sent a slave
to each man's yoke,
oil press and furrow,
to free for toil the free Greek:

the free raised these!" she cried
to the blue sky and honey-
veined columns. "This is
no pyramid." And I saw
the loins and wrists
and bones and tendons of those disprized
who in absence reared the great frieze.

When the Five Prominent Poets

gathered in inter-admiration
in a small hotel room, to listen
to each other, like Mme. Verdurin
made ill by ecstasy,
they dropped the Muse's name.
Who came.

It was awful.
The door in shivers and a path
plowed like a twister through everything.
Eyeballs and fingers littered that room.
When the floor exploded the ceiling
parted
and the Muse went on and up; and not a sound
came from the savage carpet.

Gentle Reader

Late in the night when I should be asleep
under the city stars in a small room
I read a poet. A poet: not
a versifier. Not a hot-shot
ethic-monger, laying about
him; not a diary of lying
about in cruel cruel beds, crying.
A poet, dangerous and steep.

O God, it peels me, juices me like a press;
this poetry drinks me, eats me, gut and marrow
until I exist in its jester's sorrow,
until my juices feed a savage sight
that runs along the lines, bright
as beasts' eyes. The rubble splays to dust:
city, book, bed, leaving my ear's lust
saying like Molly, yes, yes, yes O yes.

PART FOUR

1 9 7 0

1 9 7 5

The Shade-Seller

For A. R. Ammons

"Sombra?"
he asked us from his little booth. And shade
we bought to leave our car in.

By noon
the sand was a mealy fire; we crossed by planks
to the Revolcadero sea.

One day
we were later and hotter; and he peered out
and "No hay sombra!" he told us.

That day
when we came back to our metal box, frightened
we breathed for a terrible instant

the air
fiery and loud of the hooked fish.
Quick! Quick! Our silver key!

Sometimes
now I dream of the shade-seller; from his dark
he leans, and "sombra . . ." I tell him.

There is
candescent sand and a great noise of heat
and it is I who speak that word

heavy
and wide and green. O may he never
answer my one with three.

Dishwasher as Absolution

Red-eyed as Rikki-Tikki glows
her roaring cyclops.
In the fairest sky
the stars come out; still the dark grows.

As bone shined white or shell shined pink,
shriven by motion,
through sudsy tumult
shut in their steamy cell her dishes wink.

On the town dump, she thinks, fire flares;
ants clean a starfish
in the green Antilles;
in Guanajuato vultures ride the airs.

Fish pare the drowned, the fisher cleans his catch;
the slow earth wheels
toward the middle waste:
she leans against the windowsill to watch.

The roar goes into silence, with a click:
the electric sum of absolution
or solution
has appeased the yellow plates' arithmetic.

The red eye shuts; but the stars stand in the bough.
Under the tap
she washes her hands, her hands—
but it is not easy, and nothing tells her, Now!

The Travelers

Up from the city street, as in any green wood,
the leaves came out, the red sun sank and died.
On that spring evening we breasted as we could
the brutal breakers of the decibel tide.

There was a lady, and a gentleman, there
at opposite ends of the room, unintroduced,
discrete, who, some of us knew, would make a pair
on a common trip before the leaves were loosed.

She managed a martini with finesse,
he shielded a gin-and-tonic from the smother;
no one elbowed through that press
to bring one up to face the other.

We, uncommitted, felt the isolation
of landlubbers who meet the sea:
joined in our minds by their common destination,
they seemed apt for travelers' company.

But at the very quay, which would go
first aboard, in what style, with what commissions,
delays, friends—no one could truly know
with certainty; not even their own physicians.

Pondicherry Blues

(FOR VOICE AND SNARE-DRUM)

Mrs. Pondicherry was/ fat and mean,
she had four/ pug/ dogs and a limousine
black/ as West Virginia coal;
and she troubled herself about her soul,
yes, she surely was concerned/ about her soul.

Father O'Hare was thin as a steeple,
the poor and the lonely were his passion and his people.
Pondicherry would ask/ that man to come to dinner
and talk/ to him/ about The Sinner.
And Father O'Hare got very/ very/ tired of Mrs. Pondicherry,
he got raw-/ bone/ tired of Pondicherry.

She changed her will like/ she changed her furs
cause she surely did know that they both were hers,
and she drove that man beside himself
with her wills/ and her pelts/ and her pugs/ and her pelf,
she drove him purely beside himself.

One day she was sitting on her velvet seat
her mink/ round her shoulders and her footstool for her feet
and a cushion for/ each/ pug;
and her heart gave a leap and she fell on the rug,
she fell/ right/ down/ on her big/ red/ rug.

They put her into/ bed and called Father O'Hare
but he couldn't get there and he couldn't get there
and she lay on her bed for a/ solid/ hour
and she didn't say a word cause she didn't own the power,
didn't own the power to say/ a single word.

Her mind was thin and cold as a hag,
in her eyes was a beggar with a/ bowl and a rag,
and her ears/ heard/ a cold/ wind start
to blow the trash round the alleys of her heart,
to blow/ cold/ trash round the gutters of her heart.

But Father O'Hare he was/ serving the poor,
he never reached the house and he never crossed the door
till she closed her eyes and/ she stopped her breath
in the lonesome/ slum/ of death
that dark/ trashy/ street of/ death.

Linkwood Road

The old lady walking, wears gloves. It is a shady
93 and the dogs' tongues drip. The old gentleman under
the dazed tree wears a jacket and, yes, a vest, and shined
black shoes. It is enough to break out flags about.

Surely they must die, of sunstroke, one, and of suffocation, the other.
In the meantime, what a fury of purpose and coolness:
who would trust the surgeon-of-crisis, in shorts?
Unthinkable the *corrida,* without the suit of lights.

It is doubtful that the old lady has a fitting destination;
the old gentleman is reading the obituary of a younger friend. That
white glove can be seen in the private dark, lessening its confusion,
and the jacket is comprehensible to the threatening mirror, and to all
matadors.

The Clock

This stream of energy must be regulated . . . It is
done by a process of division. THE BOOK OF CHANGES

My clock jumped on cement.
The hands flew off.
Folded like yes
they settled at the bottom of the glass.
It was not dead.
I put it to my ear and tick it said.

It never stops. I wind
because it ticks.
It ticks because I wind;
its face is equal everywhere and blind.
It cannot mark
its light, separate its dark from all dark.

Though I was shrewd and knew
a thing or two,
lies lies it fed
me first: "salvation through division" what it said,
and gave to each
that identical portion no event could teach.

Love's lost extent, or fear's
gross minute
it equated.
That immaculate count related
figures to space,
both to its own unalterable base.

The hands agree:
we are in time;
even detached, believe
in synchronicity.
This handless clock and I have come
jointly to terms.

In joy and terror
I move in time where
nothing points to error;
I move in space
where love's event,
and death's, notch
time's face.

Notes toward Time

I

The mad have nightmares. When
they wake
they find
their dream beside them.
Tense. But no present or past.

II

He cannot bear the dust's word.
She loves what dies.

What dies is unbearable
to her. What dies is what he loves.

The plastic rose
affronts. Only the falling

is bright. Falling
affronts. What goes was never true.

The rose affronts the light
by falling apart. Precious because

it falls, the rose rebukes
what stays.

The schizoid heart tells
what is alive, by its dying.

III

At a high inn in
a pinpoint angle near Trapani
in Sicily I came into

a cold room, this was dusk,
empty except for Miss
Judy Garland in a small brown box,
singing, singing
that's what I call
Balling
the Jack.

IV

A limited number of moons emerge.
Let us forget constantly that the planet's
turn is ours; our quiddity
begins and ends everything. Come here:
in our usual bodies, create the future and past,
bird and moon.

V

Help! While we slept débris has been emptied upon us:
blank hours like loops of undeveloped film
have littered us, a pile beyond belief; foxed chatter,
rusted conclusions, non-returnable affections. O the noise!
They will kill us, or anyway smother us from blue air.
There is a motion,
make it with me and we are elsewhere,
unscratched, silent as a leaf.

VI

In Erice stone is cold.
The usual angels tell the time by sun.
In the cold cleft the jackdaw tells the sun,
in the bronze cup the clapper tolls the moon.
Time stands between the angel and its angle.

The plastic rose is time's nightmare.
Take it in your hand, turn it
to petals fronting the light.
These stone garlands light the morning, empty the dusk.
The bare high country calls its seasons home.

The planet's motion holds the nest in stone,
the bronze bell tells the rose to fall apart.
Not numberless, our hours turn the earth:
the angel's eyes are blank, but in our sun
the stone sings, silent as a leaf.

Mr. Mahoney

Illicitly, Mr. Mahoney roams.
They have him in a room, but it is not his.
Though he has become confused, it is not in this.
Mr. Mahoney cannot find his room.

A young blond nurse gentles him by the elbow.
I hear her again in the hall: "Mr. Mahoney,
this isn't your room. Let's go back and see
if you've brushed your teeth. Yours is *820*."

Why brushing his teeth is the lure, I cannot say.
Does he prize it so? She darts on white feet
to spear him from strange doors; I hear her repeat
with an angel's patience, "Yours is down *this* way."

But 820 is a swamp, a blasted heath.
A dozen times returned, he knows it is wrong.
There is a room in which he does belong.
He has been to 820; he has brushed his teeth.

Before his biopsy, the harried nurses attest,
Mr. Mahoney was tractable in 820,
though very old and brown. He will have to go;
this is not the hall, not the building for his quest.

Tranquilized, Mr. Mahoney still eludes.
At 2 A.M. in my dark 283
the wide door cracks, and sudden and silently
Mr. Mahoney's nutty face obtrudes.

It is gently snatched back by someone behind it.
"That is someone *else's* room. Yours is this way,
Mr. Mahoney." He could not possibly stay.
He is gone by noon. He did not have time to find it.

Trial Run

But I think that things are the same with many today as they were in
Noah's time, when he built the Ark of planks and timbers: for none of the
workmen and carpenters who fashioned it were saved.

PIERS PLOUGHMAN

They saw it take the water—the finished Ark,
after that long ridiculous procession:
the question-mark giraffe, the elephant
waving its ears, placing its plushy foot;
the loose-lip goat burning its yellow eye.
It floated, worthy, tight as you could ask.

Even where they watched, clotted on the top rocks,
would be a shining welter in, say, another hour:
not one green thing to clutch at as they went,
but water down upon them, up, to catch them—
the liquid howl of chaos, carrying
that tight right bark with all its procreant freight.

On the last sunny day (caulking the seams,
the green trees like a fleet of anchored clouds
above them; the crucial frame, the smell of shavings,
and the honor of accuracy, under the sweet blue
sky, paling, paling), they had understood
the only part of them to go would be the job.

It seemed unfair, but no more arguable
than the waters and the rough great wind.
And one, at least, just as the first cold hand
of water took his ankle, had a thought
that he would rather see her ride there, his,
still faintly seen, than, rocking in her hold

stand docile on commissioned planks.
She would bear it out, he knew, with bleat
and grunt and howl, and—doves being doves—
one might find out a green tree or its leaf.
In any case, it rode so as to argue
some future fortune for a carpenter.

The Fittest

When the great dust
has settled, settled completely
and the air
completely is soundless,
he will be there.
In his neat thousands
will move.

Poor cockroach
he will be blind,
not sterile. His seed, his galaxy
of seed
will shine and rustle,
blind but agile.

Where a child's elbow
curved, where a man
spoke and moved
where bird and woman sang
will come his shining rustle:
where the rose
sprang from its green stem.

Food

A woman of the more primitive tribes
of Eskimo, concerned with nourishment,
cooked with heather clawed out from under snow;

mittens too precious, tore the heather loose
in that weather. The bare malformed hands,
nails curved, grew flesh like smoked wood.

Under an open sky, such fuel burned too fast;
in the snow-house, the walls would soften—
worse, smoke trouble the house's master.

She lay, low, to cook in a flat hut with a hole
in its roof. Blow! Blow! The ashes flew
into her mane, her red mongoose eyes.

To eat is good. To trap, to kill, to drive
the dogs' ferocity is heroic to tell:
full-bellied sagas' stuff.

The clawing for heather, the black curved nails,
cramped breath for smoke, smoke for breath,
the witch mask clamped on the bride face

bring nothing, but life for the nourished.
Poor cannibals; we eat what we can:
it is honorable to sustain life.

By her breath, flesh, her hands, no
reputation will be made, no
saga descend. It is only the

next day made possible.

Reading Aloud at Dusk

The small blind cripple's face was ready:
raised to receive the host of Mrs. Eddy.

Before the narrow house was tender dusk.
The dahlia-colored cat named Cheops licked his chops,

came into the room to the wheelchair and its dapper
sitter magnificent and fragile as a grasshopper.

A flower, alive, with an African name, grew noiseless
in a pot near my hand that held the printed voice.

I read how matter, how sin, is nothing, is not,
and Cheops unbuttoned his eyes behind my back;

the orange tom's squint face lit that dusk like a moon;
but the blind clear eyes stared straight through the room;

the blind clear eyes went forth to battle matter,
to liquidate the mantel   the pain   the table   the terror.

Never made flesh, the pure word rang like steel,
the corrupt clock ticked its tick and darkness fell.

A single roller-skate scoured the street and hushed;
the dark full violet rumpled its flowery flesh.

Pinned down in blackness, bright as a butterfly's flicker
she plunged her gleam like a knife in the void of matter;

washed with Mary Baker's smile the crucifix
to cleanse the shadow from the empty sticks.

It Is the Season

          when we learn
or do not learn
to say goodbye . . .

The crone leaves that, as green
virgins, opened themselves
to sun, creak at our feet

and all farewells return
to crowd the air:
say, Chinese lovers by a bridge,

with crows and a waterfall;
he will cross
the bridge, the crows fly;

children who told each other
secrets, and will not speak
next summer.

Some speech of parting
mentions God, as in
a Dieu, Adios,

commending what cannot
be kept
to permanence.

There is nothing of north
unknown, as the dark
comes earlier. The birds

take their lives in their wings
for the cruel trip.
All farewells are rehearsals.

Darling, the sun rose
later today.
Summer, summer

is what we had.
Say nothing yet.
Prepare.

How We Learn

Plurality in death
fogs our mind.
One man tries to breathe
in a sealed mine:
this is how we learn.
Eye to eye.

Corporate guilt, plague,
tidal wave, we make our
sluggish guess.
But the dead child in the ditch.
O yes.

At the siege of Stalingrad
an old man starving
ate his pet cat.
Later in the hall
hanged himself, because

after that meal
he looked around to find
all in its place;
his cat no longer there.
And he still was.

Spread of Mrs. Mobey's Lawn

On Mrs. Mobey's lawn
Deer is near Squirrel,
who's neighbored by
Rooster; Black Man, Rooster's size,
all red lips and white eyeballs stands also.

Speed is cast fast
in iron. Nuts are stored
in absentia. Squirrel
rears up solid; proud lust
treads only cut grass where
no hen errs.

Black small Man pops his look.
His lips and Rooster's comb
the same hard red.
Mrs. Mobey has flight,
providence, potency,
service, all arrested.

Faster than grass
grows Mrs. Mobey's lawn:
its iron-peopled stillness
advances acre by acre.
Deer, Squirrel, Rooster, Man
move iron towards us.

The Sea Fog

It was sudden.
That slightly heaving hotel, from a folder,
was there one instant: through the glass a bloodorange ball
just diving, a pure blue desert of dusk
on the other horizon: a motion, the symbol of seas;
music, and drinks, and the self-conscious apparel,
the relative facets, of steward and poster, and sun-disc
just hidden.

The ship spoke
with a minotaur sound from around and under,
and we raised our eyes: but the sea was gone:
sub-sun, the peel of moon, the plausible shift
of dunes of water, our precious image of movement—
gone, gone, clean gone. The fog was at the pane.
No shore behind us; ahead in the breathy drift
no port.

Supported
by shore and port, now we had neither.
There was only here. The ship was here
in the fog. The ship roared and the fog blotted
us into itself and whirled into its rifts,
and the sealess skyless fear—and there was fear—
had nothing to do with sinking—at least, not
into water.

Worse:
when we went below, at the familiar turn
a bulkhead reared instead, metal and huge—
and trapped, we turned from that hulk and hastened
through stranger stairs and came from a different angle
to a cabin stiller and smaller though none of its objects had moved.
But the mirror stirred like fog when we looked for the fastened face.

We crept
through fog all night but it closed behind us:
around and very close above:
only below in the black the self-lit fishes
passed ignorantly among the wrack of wrecks
and all the water held its tongue and gave
no password. And so sealed in our silent passage
we slept.

The bell
for the bulkhead doors to open, woke us.
Everything had been reconnected: sun to the sea,
ship to the sun, smiles to our lips, and our names related
to our eyes. Who could—in that brassy blue—
have stillness to harbor the memory
of being relative to nothing; isolated;
responsible?

Simon

I do what Simon says.
But the voice, quick and muffled,
gives some orders
which are not Simon's.

Simon I try to please.
It is necessary, and right, too, but
there is the doubt if
Simon has said, or has not.

Did Simon say, *Do that,* or
did that come Simonless
from the quick voice, the soft
instruction? Perhaps a bad mistake.

If Simon has not said it,
what then? Jumbled together: *Live, Die;*
which was authentic Simon? *Go. Come.*

Distinguish, Simon says.

Language as an Escape from the Discrete

I came upon two wasps
with intricate legs all occupied.
If it was news communicated,
or if they mated or fought,
it was difficult to say of that clasp.

And a cold fear because I did not know
struck me apart from them, who moved,
whose wasp-blood circulated,
who, loveless, mated, who moved;
who moved and were not loved.

When the cat puts its furred illiterate
paw on my page and makes a starfish,
the space between us drains my marrow
like a roof's edge. It drinks milk,
as I do; one of its breaths is final.

And even the young child, whose eyes
follow what it speaks, to see in yours
what it will mean, is running away
from what it sent its secret out to prove.
And the illiterate body says hush,

in love, says hush; says, whatever
word can serve, it is not here.
All the terrible silences listen always; and hear
between breaths a gulf we know is evil.
It is the silence that built the tower of Babel.

The Dream Habitués

Odd we've never met there,
spending all that time.
But then, it's a big country.

Erratic, too, as to lighting and climate.
Will it be crowded,
or the reverse? Tiresome, as to entry?

Yet I keep going back. God knows how often,
if I added up. Which means
I ought to know a fair-

sized group. But the people move about so.
And total strangers accost you,
looking familiar.

And the transportation!
Take you off to see a ruin, or cave,
and forget you. That's at its worst.

Yes, I've had incidents
curl the hair on my head.
But then at its best

how marvelous . . . I had a dance
there once more like, well,
swimming? or flying? No. Nothing I'd learned.

A couple of bad experiences.
And one doesn't know,
so to speak, which way to turn,

But then that can happen—
or something almost like it—
in any city. The closest shave.

And, if one wishes,
one can always wake.
Or, so far, I have.

The Things

My mother's gold serpent bit its tail.
Its tiny rubies stared along its back
to the flat gold head that held themselves.
All gold, and meaning forever.

Lopsided in red chalk, still the heart
under the feet is pierced by a smudged
red crooked arrow: clearly meaning
impacted pain, or pleasure.

Thing made word—blameless uncheating
speech: clear as those hasty sticks
the soldier crossed and held, high
in the rosy smoke for Joan.

Rainy Night at the Writers' Colony

Dead poets stalk the air,
stride through tall rain and peer
through wet panes where
we sleep, or do not, here.

I know the names of some
and can say what they said.
What do we say worth the while
of the ears of the dead?

I know who shook marred
fruit of difficult bough
and from the rank discard
salvaged enough.

The rain stops; at two
the moon comes clear.
What they did, we know.
It is we who are here.

Naked under their eye,
we—honest, grave, greedy,
pedant, fool—lie
with what we make of need.

The Provider

The night the flowers were butchered
I was gone.
Some sort of harvest comes
to everything nurtured.

But now who has the flesh, the wine
for days grown harder?
Out of this larder
will frost drink, and dine?

Now that his butcher's glance
stores blackness and pallor
will he swallow raw color?
Gnaw on fragrance?

I was not there; but have known
this slaughter, of old.
I know quite well the night, cold;
the knife, honed.

Good Fortune of Pigeons

For Arthur Gregor

There is a dead pigeon hung
upside down in the bare big tree.
Around, about, flying out, in,
sidling, shooting their necks,
claws curved for balance,
conversing
steadily in soft glottals, are perhaps
a hundred pigeons.

Over wine and bread, a jug of daffodils,
inside the open window
we watch. Spring is still invisible
but the air is full of it, boiling in boughs.
We are shocked at such poise.

Why not another tree? Or at least
a decent distance? But no, all around
murmur and clean themselves
the wise and terrible pigeons,
saying, in throaty pigeon English:
Never mind.
Never

mind.

Margins of Choice

The doomed gunman, surrounded,
arranges
his ammunition within reach, uses
his knees in the best way, adjusts his range.

The gardener cuts all the flowers, heaps
colors;
carries them off under the killer
frost's moon eye,
to die warm.

The man dying alters his pillow's angle,
shifts his gaze,
motions "no" with his finger, lays down
that hand; shuts, opens
his eyes.

So, as death quiet as the scent
of earth
moves closer, armed
with his only weapon,
separation,

I close with you, touch your skin,
your lips;
wake earlier, or lie awake,
look at you, look;
allocate
my instants'
shadowy heap.

Country Drive-In

Sudden around the curve a high-up and huge
face luminous as a clock blocks out a quarter-sky.
Small I move small in my small car below
the head of a giantess, unbodied as John's
on the screen's charger.
Blue as seas, its eyes release bright pools,
kidney-shaped tears slide down the vasty cheeks.
The lips' cavern parts on teeth
whiter and bigger than any bedded wolf's.
How can I fit her mammoth grief
into the dark below my matchstick ribs?

Carney Elegy

For John

The Indestructible Girl spun on a wheel:
she was not ugly, and looked destructible enough,
flattened and flying; and the Fire Eater, her young man,
ate fire: flames shot like promises between his lips.

The Barker barked, but silent as the tiger
they spun and blazed—the single silent tiger,
carrying his flame deep in his eyeballs and shallow on his hide;
the chic zebra, silent in his stripes.

And near us, and silent too, death, conventionally invisible.
The straw burned dusty under hoof and heel, the sun sucked motes
into the air to turn there and burn. We amicable
three, between the Barker and the fusty tent.

If that third member, if the guest, had spoken,
what should we then have said to one another:
Goodbye? I love you? Or both?
No more than whirling girl, fiery boy, tiger, zebra, straw,

New Hampshire July stubble, did we speak—to each other, that is.
As for love: this was our closest moment, or so I now say.
As for goodbye, my vanished circus friend—did the Fire Eater
say that, to the Indestructible Girl?

Elective Affinities

What a curious rendezvous: through mean sleet
down this straight street over corrupted snow
you travel travel to me. We never meet.

Shrilled from the dream of ease at this outrageous hour with a jolt,
when even cold schoolrooms sleep, you mine the dark
to sling your anti-gospel at my double-bolt.

What wretched congress: I light the sacred flame
under the coffee, listen, shiver in my wool,
and *Slackk!* comes the missile in this insane game.

You will miss your sleep, hate me, be stupid though not innocent:
or, industrious, you will be honored by the Horatio Alger Club,
which says you will grow up to be our President.

Like a terrier I am on my diet of silliness and rape,
of murder most detailed; of a page of the dead's living faces:
a Buyer, a Broker, a Rotarian, and a Landscape-

Architect, who will buy, broke, rotate,
or scape nothing further. Someone is led away
in handcuffs. I spill coffee on a Head of State.

I don't even know your name. "Your Morning Eagle boy"
says your Christmas card, five days in advance,
wishing me, via a Lamb, all Peace and Joy

now, and in the New Year. In which, you'll be back
and I'll lie in wait for what we'll both have learned
that will alter ourselves, before tomorrow's *Slackk!*

The Arrivals

My dead are shining like washed gold.
Like gold from what-you-will freed:
cobwebs, mold, rust, the anonymous mud—
and plunged in the icy waver of water
to flash at the hot sun.

They come shining happily inside a moment
translated only now so long after.
They arrive in the comfort of comrades and a
nimbus of silence.

Accurate and able they shine
in ordinary glory
cleared from the clock's confusion that held them
distant, aghast.

The Gesture

In winter the house, which sits on rock,
braced on a granite ledge,
is a web naked to shock;
a web of boards; eaves at the wind's edge.

Like wind the snow is shredded through nettles,
the rock humps huge under the granulate
sweep. Inside the house, the mouse rattles
rapidly in the lathes, and the spider's mate

hangs by moonlight in the midst of her own construction.
The months' names then are northern January, February, March.
Dust grows out of itself, and the sun
comes, if at all, in a knife's shape, thin, very sharp.

When the wheels bring voices the house, breached and entered,
appears as constant in its steady office:
the shrunk spider is the spit of her progenitors;
no change is apparent in the generations of the mice.

Then comes that season blue and green and limber
when the humans laugh and eat; make love; go, come.
Summer by summer—long, long in the mouse's number,
a flash in the rock's—they count to their anonymous sum.

The voices are set, distinct, in the cave of all silence,
as the rose and green are set now on the apple's icy bark.
The rock is a pebble's flash in the earth's summer;
the earth is a flash in the huge caves of the dark.

But something here rips out of its sequence,
will not feed and follow the sum of the mouse and the spider,
the rock. It is a gesture; a specific, chance
gesture. It belongs without end to its lover.

The Rock-Plant Wife

The rock-plant wife is dead.
She failed to overwinter.
Along with the rare peony and most
of the candy-tuft
she is gone.

A cell bloomed in her body,
one icy night, hoped in her warmth
and was not disappointed;
sent its seed along her flesh,
its garden; like clover
took over that small space.

Now she herself is planted like a bulb.
Three of my friends are down there since first snow,
in that great soil where roots and rocks
and friends lie turning
with my turning world,
but do not turn to me.

The rock-plant husband moves among the rocks.
He could not keep his wife or peony.
He sends his spade into the shallow mound
for my dwarf-iris clump
and says her name to me
while friends of mine turn
silently in deeper soil.
I touched them, and they, me. We had
kisses and arguments and silences, all different.
Now I have the last.

The clump is up,
blue as our summer day.
He, like any gardener,
believes in spring. I simply say
(*pace* the gardener) in summer—
spring is too far.

Short Views in Africa

The elephant
comes past the Visitor two feet away,
watched through the blind's
chink. His shoulder strides,
he places like plush a foot,
then another.
The tufted tail goes by.

High up, at night, the Visitor sees
the herd come out:
singly, in moonlight, from the bush, the trees
by twos; in a file of huge three;
scoop mud, blow, breathe. 103 elephants.

The Visitor
is healed by elephants,
pretends they will stay; falls asleep
kneeling at the sill. At four
the Visitor's eyes open:
the herd, rocking and shifting,
blowing, putting plashy feet,
is preparing to leave.
When the sun wakes her
they are somewhere else.

II

The best surprise is death.
She dreaded this
but it fits lightly. Even the frantic spurt,
ripped flank, snapped neck
settle so easily to: rock,
gold grass, stubble, bones, bones.

Everywhere, bones.
Simple, the bones of beasts.
This is the short view,
like a cut nerve—peace.
The bones are everywhere like grace
in the early sun.

III

The long, warped triangle
of the giraffe's pretty face,
the paintbrush lashes, the roving head
over the thornbush cruise, shy and leafy.
This air is pure with the ignorance of death.

Cat-lax the lion blinks
in noon's thin shade.
Lioness raises her head, stares,
lowers it; in a heap
the cubs are burrowed, dazed
with red food.

The skeletons inside the warm fur
go by paces, by springs, by stalks,

to their final sun;
to light, wind, grass.
Knowledgeable,
the Visitor watches the lions.

IV

In Olduvai are the bones
that block the way to ignorance.
Which bones, which minute first
looked on death and said, "That
belongs to me." Then said, then later said,
" . . . belongs to what I love."

The Visitor can imagine herself—
imagines herself—
into the short sunny view;
bones unrelated, messageless,
the million bones benevolently whitening,
crying nothing
but hunger and motion;
not secretive of the permanent desire; not
saying
Mary Ann Kelly, Beloved.
Xenophon lies here.
I was Hannah.

v

Well. Bless the giraffe,
the elephant, the lioness, the short
blessed view.

Kneel at the window.
Wait under the thorntree
for the sun. Go away
carrying your difference, you cannot leave it.
Say, Not God
himself would dare to lay it on you without
relief.
Tell your secret bones: Wait.

The Monosyllable

One day
she fell
in love with its
heft and speed.
Tough, lean,

fast as light
slow
as a cloud.
It took care
of rain, short

noon, long dark.
It had rough kin;
did not stall.
With it, she said,
I may,

if I can,
sleep; since I must,
die.
Some say,
rise.

The Terrible Naïve

sleepwalk, feed
birdseed to kittens,
dislike arithmetic of
courtesy;

omnipotently shrewd
will whistle
in mirrors; will wrestle,
but only after

securely lashing
your wrists with
their tough
vulnerability;

execute ambushes
with un-
loaded guns, but when
they cry

"I die! I die!"
the dark flood
is your
blood.

A Motel in Troy, New York

A shadow falls
on our cribbage. The motel window
is a glass wall down to grass.

A huge swan
is looking in: cumulus-cloud body,
thunder-cloud dirty neck

that hoists the painted face
coral and black. Inky eyes
peer at our lives.

It cannot clean its strong
snake neck. It stands
squat on its yellow webs

splayed to hold
scarcely up the heavy
feathered dazzle.

All of us stare. Then
in a lurch it turns
and waddles rocking,

presses the stubble to the tip
of the blue pond. Sets sail
in one pure motion

and is received by distance.
That crucial soiled snake neck
arched to a white high curve

received by distance
and the shadowy girl
across the water.

Over Timberline

It was never the air
betrayed them:
cloud-field, cloud-tower
or turret, shining
their wings that glitter
as they tilt. Air
held them like a comet in its course.

Earth was their enemy,
mother turned fury
to her strayed children:
gravity's anger, to call
them home in a long scream.

So a red scrap of cloth
whipped in the peak's breath
which no breath answers,
flays fast; over stone
the ants go their bright cold
ways; clouds join and part,
stunted green darkens
and shines and darkens.

Softly

Wherever we walk, we walk
over the silent. Cities
we know or never heard of,

whose citizens gave themselves
in sleep to dreams not understood,
saw how far the stars were
and how the moon shrank and went.

Dust to dust, they coupled,
joined dust they found precious,
lit fires for cold and dark,
lost what they could not keep.

Walk softly over the dust of their cities
deep below, over the places
that were dear to them, or bitter,
under the pasture, the forest

the ugly street, the museum
that houses their artifacts,
in respect of that fraternity.
Over its numbers, see how few move.

Interrogation

All day
and sometimes in the hollow evening
in their tunnels the machines
have questioned me:
heart, belly, skull.
"Don't breathe . . ." they said.
Click. "Breathe . . ."
They had it their way.

Flat on the silver
surface or up
against the shiny plate: "Don't
breathe . . ." Count. Click.
"Breathe." Not an inch's
shelter.

Now they know
nothing, nothing.
I gave my name, rank,
social security number.
They have all the sights.
I, the secrets.
Breathing, or not,
I have told them nothing. Nothing.

A Dream of Games

I   A GAME OF SCRABBLE

His fingers hesitate over
his row—it is stammering
with i   i   i. Here nothing can stand
alone, let alone i.
Insipid, he finally puts
and judgment
leaps on the board with a sweep.

The tall child makes *gory*, doubled.
The smooth tiles spell
relationships, accidents.
...*eath*, ...*eath*. Fingering
a *d*, one pauses here. A *d*
would do; *br* would be better.

Beyond the balcony the sea
flees in long quivers. Now here is the *q*,
Friday before Crusoe—he has used his *u*
in *ruins*.
Below, slick and lovely, the frangipani
boughs black as snakes and bare, spring
into pink at the top. Has anyone ever made
frangipani?

She has ...*ight;* the sea suggests
an *l*—the sailboats shed it, the mango shines it back,
br the mango says. She has only an *n*
and the whole island disappears: where is the moon?
Not one thin star? *Delight*'s chance is lost.

Instead, *gone* appears; then *vein,*
now *vasty.* Everything stops
for argument. *Vasty?* Halls, halls
of death, says the woman, wringing her rings.
The sun drops a little, but *vasty*
is removed, and there is *video.* Two tiles
are left, *e, r,* and go on *lied.* The man says
that is foreign, the woman says
songs are here. There is no dictionary.
Lieder stays.

The woman has won. The child is sad. The man
looks at the words, connected, without context.
On the rail
the tiny dragon, alligator, lizard
over his eyes' black specks, smiles
and *lieder, death, vein, night*
just as the sun makes its move
to leave, shatter and meld and clatter
into the box.

II   A BRIDGE OF KNAVES

Knave says the book: *slippery,*
a shrewd fellow. Here, all dignity
stuffily clad, in profile or not quite,
hunts with the pack;

falls with no sound face-
down on felt. Lifted,
takes on his rank, jaunty, reticent;
looks past the players.

Christened a club, so is he dark,
time-out-of-mind, if dates matter. Club?
He prefers to claim deep chairs, deep rugs,
hot andirons, snow beyond glass; exclusions;

but his half-turn still says, too,
old caves, old hunts, new hunts; egg-shell
heads, egg-shell bones. Say what he will
he stays the ancient heir.

The Diamond Knave that points
his almost-smile, says, glitter
on velvet or flesh like velvet; cut
or be cut. True, rain and sun

fling *trompe-l'oeil* imitations,
flash-and-go, and bastard cousins,
terrapin, rattler, carry
that family insignia.

The lips of the Knave of Hearts tilt
up. What he has is different.
He cannot set a necklace, break
a head, play the grave-digger;

variety is his claim. He says
his 3-inch sac will give you
an empire, a suicide; says it
has the ultimate connections, last and first.

Three Knaves know how absurd
is the fourth's eminence:
Spade must be the dealer's irony;
yokel, upraised.

The root's, the earthworm's visitor,
the flower's clownish uncle.
But in cardboard, one-eyed and natty,
In the end, he says, depend on me.

III   A DREAM OF GAMES

The game is dreamed for the rules:
when dusk takes the green diamond
set in dust, even the players' ghosts
are gone: the three-bat swing; the ghost

that hitched its belt, its cap; dipped
for the resin, hid its paw; leaned
like a pointer toward the tools-
of-ignorance crouch. In dark the rules wait it out.

The game we dream writes lines
where *love* means *nothing,* and *service*
is neither waiter, priest nor stallion,
and *let* is a net's whisper.

The game is dreamed for the rules.
Monte Alban's old rule dreamed
that ball-court from which the loser died.
Chaos, soft idiot, is close

as breath. But the games appear,
celestial in order; contracts we make
with light: the winner humbled,
the loser connected with his law.

The Sisters

Everyone notices they are inseparable.
Though this isn't quite so, it might well be.
Talk about depending on each other . . .
One can't say they are totally
congenial—irritation isn't unknown.

Yet it is, truly, touching, how they go on
year after year, not just pairing lives but
taking even holidays and vacations together,
sharing what happens to come along.
Here they are in the Caribbean.

Choose a day—the eighteenth of March for example:
they awake at almost but not quite
the same instant, disoriented:
where is the east? where anything else?
But they aren't going to dog each other all day.

B, anyone would have to admit,
is the better adjusted—easily pleased.
What marvelous lobster! she cries.
Smell the air! (The island is full of spices
and the air is soft as well as fragrant.)

A's energy always seems to be erratic:
first she's on and on about something,
then she wants a nap. She's a great sleeper
and has been known to cast away
hour after precious hour asleep without shame.

And she gets fixations—dashing off
to some spot they've already seen,
and talking about it when she gets back.
Take the little group of graves by the Old Men's Home
the station-wagon passes on its way to the beach.

Both of them noticed it—how could they help?
It's a little patch, unfenced, with four or five
graves. One apparently new and covered
with brightness. They even both waved
to the four old men on the porch who waved back.

But later, it turns out, *A* went back by herself,
sharp-eyed as ever, to examine the yellow
and violet cellophane, the rubber pond-lilies
floating on dust; the whole glittering heap
of rainbow mound; even asked questions.

That happened this morning; with the result
that when *B* swam in the sea—that sea
like a sapphire flawed with gold and green—
A went to sleep. The time she wastes
like that, slack as a weed in a wave!

This means that tonight she'll keep *B* awake
probably for hours, prowling about.
But they fight less than most sisters
and when the question of separation once arose
you should have seen them recoil—both, both.

At Scrabble this afternoon they played partners:
tiles smooth to the fingertips, words appearing,
solid as objects—*salmon, cat;* or abstract,
as *who, why, go.* They did very well.
Then *A* wouldn't participate in the talk at dinner.

On the whole, this was a good day; hard rain
rattled the roof, then the real rainbow threw up its arch,
and amicably they watched the blood-orange dip
into water; then stars, larger and brighter than elsewhere.
Before bed, *A* looked at herself in the mirror, using *B*'s eyes.

The Birthday Party

The sounds are the sea, breaking out of sight,
and down the green slope the children's voices
that celebrate the fact of being eight.

One too few chairs are for desperate forces:
when the music hushes, the children drop
into their arms, except for one caught by choices.

In a circle gallops the shrinking crop
to leave a single sitter in hubris
when the adult finger tells them: stop.

There is a treasure, somewhere easy to miss.
In the blooms? by the pineapple-palms' bark?
somewhere, hidden, the shape of bliss.

Onto the pitted sand comes highwater mark.
Waves older than eight begin a retreat;
they will come, the children gone, the slope dark.

One of the gifts was a year, complete.
There will be others: those not eight
will come to be eight, bar a dire defeat.

On the green grass there is a delicate
change; there is a change in the sun
though certainly it is not truly late,

and still caught up in the scary fun,
like a muddle of flowers blown around.
For treasure, for triumph, the children run

and the wind carries the steady pound,
and salty weight that falls, and dies,
and falls. The wind carries the sound

of the children's light high clear cries.

Tiger

For Bessie

Diamonds or broken saucepans interchangeable,
Susie's sprung rocker, or her heart's blood,
are safe by his hatred, Tiger understands.

Tiger is Susie's dog. Tiger and Susie know
the street is wicked in old wicked ways;
the street is dangerous and covers the city.

Alley and bitch-mother are gone so long
Tiger has one live being in his city; his paws
never touch the wicked pavement

he watches. The dirt yard has a gray high
wood fence—over it fell a piece of meat rank
with poison. Susie found it first. Now she goes

into that yard with Tiger when he goes.
In his three years he hasn't seen a cat or dog
or human—wicked lives—but through the window.

The bell wheezes sometimes. Tiger flies
flies through the air, slams against the door
with 25 dog-fight noises in his teeth:

is dragged away, is shut upstairs, paces
paces paces in rage. But then blessed the bolt
shoots home, the chain jingles. Tiger shoots

down the stairs to his window, his glass; his glass
where he can watch the wicked at their ways,
who all are bad, will never be better, cannot come

in; because Tiger the Judge, unmated, single
in intent, will tear them to shreds to scatter
at Susie's cracked shoe. He has seen a dog

trotting like a Doppelgänger-enemy past and past;
or a dog in a room in the window, when at dark
the bulb is lit. His joys are Susie's step on the three steps

he has never gone down. There's a time his tongue
drips; that's summer. Then there is the time
the gas-jets on the stove stay bright all night. Tonight

snow vibrates along the street and changes it:
but not the wicked, waiting behind their walls
to rob, to murder, or to visit. The snow is like a pulse

a hypnotizing pulse. And Tiger lets himself
fall on his side by Susie's salvaged ankle
and lets the outside fill with snow and his eyes close.

The Planet

For Erlend

From the center of the Sea of Tranquility—
a dry sea and a grainy—
see shining on the air
of that stretched night, a planet.

See it as serene and bright, very bright,
a far fair neighbor;
conceive what might be there
after the furious spaces.

Green fields, green fields,
oceans of grasses, breakers of daisies;
shadows on those fields,
vast and traveling,

the clouds' shadows.
And something smaller:
in the green grass, lovers in each other's
arms, still, in the grass.

The clouds will water the fields
the stream run shining
to the sea's motion; the sea shining
as the clouds travel and shine,

so shine the daisies, as
the light in the seas
of the lovers' eyes. The innocent planet
far and simple, simple because far:

with lovers, and fields for flowers,
and a blue sky carrying clouds;
and water, water: the innocent planet,
shining and shining

Language of Moss

Secretly, the verb is changed and covered
by habit's plush and stealthy moss,
all leached, its virtue's motion gone,
only the shape left. *Fall. Go. Pass.*

To *fall* is a strange, terrible thing,
edge lost to gravity's savage reach,
what's below rushing up, nothing
between, nothing nothing to catch.

Thick tough moss cushions the plunge
of the shocked self and will not have
nonsense of risk or fracture. We say,
bland, *to fall in love.*

To *go* is to leave familiar here
for elsewhere: to another room,
street, city, tropic, tundra;
to the ashy seas that wash the moon.

But moss seals up a territory
vaster and stranger, of no fixed shape,
visa or border, In that waiting country
moss tells us, He has gone to Sleep.

As for to *pass,* it is to leave
something behind. Its motion toward
the unspecified joins itself
to the shadowy word *away.*

So two words moss captures and covers.
Strangeness, moss can and will destroy.
Now, like the unctuous men in black,
moss tells us, He has passed away.

PART FIVE

1 9 7 5

1 9 9 4

Next Summer

Catalogues of seeds flood him
in the churlish gray city weather.
Preposterous gardens, wildly catholic:
anemone, nasturtium, marigold;
roses (white red yellow) bud, uncoil,
loosen to enormous bloom. A trellis

thickens with Heavenly Blue morning
glories, black-hearted poppies burst
their furry stems, sweet alyssum snows
the border. Generous "to a fault"
are Hardy, Lavish, Profligate with Bloom,
Effortless. February's paradise.

Now, house gone for good, and garden with it,
he drops their gorgeous prophecies unopened
into trash. Not the first garden lost,
he tells himself. But all the thousand flowers
that thrust and widened from his fingers
have changed the earth, the air: bloom, stir,
invisible, busy—calling their trampling bees.

Lion under Maples

The lion, awake, is out there.
What is a lion doing under maples?
The sun catches him. She knows
the calm ferocious face set

in its monstrance of
chrysanthemum shag. The eye
is golden but too far to see.
Now there is no glimpse at all.

But she has met him before
this. And with fortune,
she will. In a clearing,
in the heat, in a wink.

Then she will be left
without fear. With great power;
everything be still,
the great head lift.

Survivor's Ballad

She's not sure if it's song or sermon,
ballad of a tightknit trio:
graduates of the Monday German,
two with beauty, and three with brio.

Three were cocky and three were witty;
two took a dim view of their local past or
future, took both to New York City.
But three times a year, they lunched at the Astor,

close as thieves in their favorite venue.
The waiter welcomed his favorite trio,
pink carnations and shiny menu:
two with beauty, and three with brio.

That was long before the trouble—
trio, carnations, wine and waiter.
The Hotel Astor has long been rubble,
she doesn't know what was built there later.

The beauties fought, and made it up;
but after that, it was *sauve qui peut*,
with more sharp cracks than a broken cup,
and she ended with double lunches *à deux*.

The dark-eyed one was put through paces
by bitter pain before she went.
The blue-eyed one lost names, then faces,
then who she was and what she meant.

Song or sermon, poet or pastor,
a dream revisits the last of the trio:
greedy and young, at the Hotel Astor,
two with beauty, and three with brio.

The Chosen

(GRENADA)

The sick are coming the sick are coming!
Today is the healing of the sick. It is
today's Good News; there has been preparation.
In this church all the chairs have arms.

Brought by the strong, the sick will come in last.
Out there the beach is a perfect blaze; no normal
rainbow ever carried more colors than this Caribbean,
and the almond blossoms are blowing; they fall

on the sand, in the wind that wildly flattens
the candle-flames in their glass. Hibiscus
is seen through the brick-lace walls, red
as the little girls' barrettes: you could go on

with the sky, and their blue ribbons; and certainly
the clouds have the same white-white as their tall socks.
The faces, color of cocoa, obsidian, sand,
of bark, of nutmeg, are turned toward the door:

the choir, quiet, seethes with intention. Now!
Between two of the strong, the sick ones creep:
lame, mostly; enormously tough and fragile,
like dark, bent-over birds. Some

spectacular ravages; but sadly, largely
it turns out, the undramatic wounds of age.
They are lowered into chairs with dignity.
A tiny old woman chatters, chatters,

part prayers, part anecdotes to an
invisible friend. *Kumbaya!* the choir bays,
drowning the mocking-bird exulting
in health in the eucalyptus.

They lowered the leper through the roof, says the gospel,
because of the crowd. The lifted faces, intent,
savor this: part of the roof, right off—
and there is the leper! The next thing

you know, he has taken up his bed and gone
home. The faces are raised to that story.
They believe it could happen; did happen; but
will not, right now. The black tall priest,

his sash embroidered with nutmeg bursting
through its mace, says he will bring them oil,
the oil of healing; and he does, bending, huge
and gentle. *Amen! Amen! It shall be so!*

shouts the choir: *hallowed be Thy name!*
Amen! Amen! It shall be so! It has a beat
like Carnival; is a kind of road-march:
the foreheads, the palms, are raised to the oil,

a huge wave lifts the entire place:
fronds that swing in the sun, the enormous
healthy day, the loud bird
in its tree. They are healed, healed:

they understand something I cannot:
that they wait: are loved: are in the palm
of the good power that chose their affliction.
Pray for us, the priest tells them, *You are closer to God.*

The bright chatterer pushes herself up
and begins to dance: a tiny road-march jump-up;
a Sister swirls, all veil and beads, to take her
claws, and down the aisle away they go like partners.

Now the Host rises, white and round
in the beautiful long black fingers
and even the choir is stricken
silent. Given: a new Body.

Power! Kingdom! shouts the choir
suddenly, *Glory!* The guitar goes
fast and deeper. *It shall be so!*
It shall be so!
         The healthy leave first,

not to hurry the honored, in their slow
return to familiar sheets. If the terms of the contract
remain mysterious, it is signed. The chosen
wait in their chairs for those not chosen.

Leaf with Berry

At the last rock of the last ledge of the last climb,
retreat blocked, he went to the edge
to look over his days and ways.

The earth lay below in colors. He watched it
with desire, but it was spread out far
far below, and was unobtainable.

At his foot was a green thing—a leaf,
slick and single, with one red berry,
had prized open a crevice in granite.

Over timberline are no trees, no bushes,
granite only, and a tremendous wind;
but the slick soft texture of the leaf

and the slick red shape of the berry
had sprung from some seed, some kind of seed,
so he let them be there for him.

Though the wind made the sound of wolves, and sun
had not warmed the granite, he gathered
that he was to take heart.

The Steps

Over sunny earth, meadow
and forest, goes the great mock
bird-shadow, clocking its hundred miles
by instants.

This fast high shadow
means nothing. This is not real
distance. Distance is below;
steps scissor it out.
Distance is where the steps go.

Steps our proportion,
we measure as we must:
groom to bride: the refugee
in the hard road's soft dust;
the man's steps, from the cell
to the distortion
of a familiar shape, opening its metal arms.

The step is the child's
first plunging waver, face
to face with distance.
Steps took Moses to that final glance;
crossed the skull's place.

The Hooves

The serpents of summer,
winter's wolves,
as dream presences
inhabit sleep.

The train missed,
the friend vanished;
arches empty as
de Chirico's beckon

there we by no means
wish to go. Where
is the beloved? Out
of what did we make

this nocturnal land-
scape? What scraps
of simple things gone wry,
of friendly sounds

changed to the nearing
noise, the hard drum
hollow and fast
of the night's mare?

Of Pairs

The mockingbirds, that pair, arrive,
one, and the other; glossily perch,
respond, respond, branch to branch.
One stops, and flies. The other flies.
Arrives, dips, in a blur of wings,
lights, is joined. Sings. Sings.

Actually, there are birds galore:
bowlegged blackbirds brassy as crows;
elegant ibises with inelegant cows;
hummingbirds' stutter on air;
tilted over the sea, a man-of-war
in a long arc without a feather's stir.

The mockingbirds are a pair. A pair
touches some magic marrow, lends
a curious solace. "Lovers" pretends
of course an anthropomorphic care
we know is specious. This is a whim
of species. Nevertheless, they come.

One, then the other, says what it has to say,
pours its treble tricks clearer
into clear air, goes; one, and the other.
In the palms' dishevelment, the random day,
over the green hot grass, fellow to fellow:
the shadow of wings, the wing's shadow.

The Night Watchman

A small light, furtive, peers,
picks out a palm bole,
breadfruit green as a snake.
The night watchman is on his rounds, his right arm
heavy with its thousand years.

The dark keeps space behind
his left shoulder. For a moment
on my white wall in a white square
shadows of palm fronds struggle
with the invisible wind.

The Caribbean has taken back
its colors: the broken moon
scatters its steps on black. Here cocks
crow all night and dogs that slept
in the sedative sun, bark, bark, bark.

I ask of the watchman the seasoned
question: What of the night? From what
will he protect me? Other questions:
Where did she go? Is the mongoose
nocturnal? What should we have done?

Dogged as cock or dog, his light will return.
Protection! Protection? While
the thin knives of the clock
shred minute by minute, and the sea
turns over its bones?

The Dogs

It is obvious that the three brown dogs, on the beach
each day, are siblings—color of coats,
shape of head, upturned mongrel tail.

They are gritty from rolling in sand to catch
the unreachable flea; they never bark.
They come, against discouragement, to lie

in a blunt triangle close to human feet.
Sometimes by stealth they move a fraction
closer, until repulsed. All morning

unless the humans walk away or go
into the bright sea, the three brown dogs
stay there, chained by a private need.

It is not the simple communal drives:
sex, hunger, sleep. Certainly not trust:
they flinch at a sharp move. It seems

to cast the humans in some curious role
they can neither play nor comprehend:
their magnet otherness, imposed

without consent, unarticulated.
Each day, silent on the pitted sand,
like ignorant disciples, the dogs come

silently, to lie in their rough triangle.
What the humans helplessly represent
stays undefined; but the dogs arrive.

Winter's Tale

Well, why did he do it *then?* I can say,
"Sir, save my little boy ere he die . . ."
That's easy, and has been said a number of times.
You might say all the dust of the earth once said "save . . .";
but the fever failed to go away.

And with the flute-players making all that uproar
no wonder he sent them out
before that ambiguous remark about sleep.
But in that sort of sleep
the little girls who do not get up

when their hands are taken
are too numerous to mention.
As for brothers, there are many,
the limit on that relationship
is remote, not to say cloudy.

We know about being set on a brother.
Martha's brother came back to her
from the dead, but there must have been
special circumstances behind it.
Mystery, ah yes, mystery

is of course the essence,
the root and sap. How true.
And if the first person did answer
it would be no doubt with something prestigious
and monosyllabic, like a thunderclap.

Yet, when the words come out, over the heads docilely raised,
"the maiden," "my brother," "my son," a little stir
goes through the eyes and ears and hands
like wind through the driest reeds. Private memory, probably,
like a curious retrospective hope.

We Pray Most Earnestly

We pray most earnestly: our breath
goes up, to Jesus and his family. Father,
mother; sometimes St. Joseph and the Saints
get into it: *Listen to our petition.*

It always strikes me as odd; like giving
water to a fountain-cherub, or coals
to that famous place that ends in . . . castle,
while someone in a somewhere desert

tries to swallow once more, or
a blue-lipped child in an arctic
alley can't find a match;
or a skeleton stirs a garbage can.

The swindler, the cop whose heart
is in his night-stick; the candy-hand
of the molester; the boys who
work the torture cells, and happily eat;

the poisoner, betrayer, rapist; oafs
whose joy is in spotting the weak; the figure
that moves in the dark, meaning ill;
those waiting to be burned alive at

6 A.M., with reason if not mercy;
sadists, patient to find
small animals; all go scatheless of our clean-faced prayers.

We pray in unison for our Bishop
(no harm in that) but have we
the time *(pray without cease-
ing).* Have we the time

for prayers that float to the vir-
tuous, the amiable with their guileless
faces; the families here
sitting in satisfaction, shoulder to shoulder?

Waking

They do not swim alone:
tricolored, the water is deep,
the invisible tide strong. They stay
near the pier. Sharks never come in.

Little Miss Piper, Mr. Pruett
with the stomach, hairy Mr. Gray,
and the children who must constantly be called back.

In the Caribbean they move in tides
come from over the bones of boys,
of girls gone down, of skeletal
galleons; the necropolis of the fish.

Out of its glitter and sparkle
they rise to the day, to the palms'
sparkle and glitter; brilliant with drops,
they step onto the ground.

So, out of the deeps of sleep
where they cannot keep company—
chosen, at least—
from the fathoms of memory, one

by one, at morning, they rise
into themselves, into their limbs, the new
sight of the old sun on their sea.
As though they would, always, wake.

Presences

Here they are common as pebbles. Tree-
frog; cat; lizard. I have been near them
today. This morning the cat, which is yellow,
trotted along the path, through the pineapple palms.

When the sun was at an angle, the lizard
espaliered against the wall's stucco, stayed
like that for minutes on end—his head
a little raised, his tail fading into nothing;

and later, by a small flashlight, I found
in its axil the tree-frog, big as a thumb,
green as green glass, pulsing with sound
so shrill it slit night's membrane like a shard.

I could have touched him. It was the same date
in history for all of us, the same acre,
the same air of spice and salt: here we were.
I do not comprehend outer space

but it is smaller, I know, than this distance
between us, this mystery we carry.
(I have seen a lioness trot like a cat,
light, light, with the tail's tip up,

I have seen the lizard's eighth cousin
rise on its alligator joints, onto tippytoes
and run fast as a dog.) But those were
in places strange to me. Here we cohabit.

The cat trots, the lizard clings to the wall,
the frog slits the silence. Close,
close, distance makes me dizzy
with its sumptuous refusals.

There is an awful grace in such mystery.
Galaxies are simpler. To have such disguises
as we circle each other: on a path,
on pink stucco; in the crotch of green.

II   THE CLOUDS

What must be said of clouds is: they are silent.
Their silence is flawless. They move
with irregular edges over the vast backdrop

steadily; or, at a moment, swiftly. A sound
would destroy that thick fleece, the puffed
and sailing curves going fast and silent.

I have seen them from above, but felt
no closer; they never promised support.
Those turreted fields are not for you.

When they tear almost imperceptibly
apart, the quiet is immense and the fila-
ments disperse and atomize.

Stained by the moon, a copper
fringe drags off the whole affair
and the moon glares round and bright

but the clouds go on away; pile white
over star over star. Release star after star.
I don't know any other choices so quiet.

When I lie flat on the ground I can feel
the stillness pass over my face. It softens
the gravestones and darkens flower faces.

Death is equally silent but does not move.
I think a good thing to see before the quiet that is
motionless, would be the bright soundless motion.

This silence fills the ear like another music.
It appeases. How much time in which to be
grateful is roughly sufficient?

III   NOW

The light in the garden has changed since death
arrived. Motionless; patient. Everything has brightened.
He had passed through, of course, leaving a bird
stiff under the nasturtiums; in a borrowed voice

called from a distant phone; that sort of thing.
But now like the stone-worn pedestal of the sundial
he is there. And what an effect on light:
the garden has taken on a gleam, a brilliance,

a flash as though the whole scene had undergone
its vernissage; the leaves glitter, separate; the flowers'
blood pulses in the petal, where lavish, grass burns
its green; the shadows are laid on with exactitude.

It is impossible to recall all the muted colors.
A blind man struck by sight could not be more astounded
than eyes that take in this meticulous riot.
It is now. And you have seen its particulars.

You Can Take It with You

For Evelyn Prettyman

2 little girls who live next door
to this house are on their trampoline.
The window is closed, so they are soundless.

The sun slants, it is going away:
but now it hits full on the trampoline
and the small figure at each end.

Alternately they fly up to the sun,
fly, and rebound, fly, are shot
up, fly, are shot up up.

One comes down in the lotus
position. The other, outdone,
somersaults in air. Their hair

flies too. Nothing, nothing, nothing can keep them down. The air
sucks them up by the hair of their heads.

I know all about what is
happening in this city at just
this moment; every last

grain of dark, I conceive.
But what I see now is:
the 2 little girls flung up

flung up, the sun snatch-
ing them, their mouths rounded
in gasps. They are there, they fly up.

The Lawn Bowlers

The clothes and the inscrutable small jack are white,
as are the dollops of cloud on the postcard-blue calm.
Not an upper stir to lift the most aerial kite;
the brilliant Green, if touched, is plush to the palm.

Over the grass toward the still, magnet jack
in a fine soundlessness the dark bowls spin
furiously: one goes clear of the pack,
delicately to touch and nestle in.

With a ritual recurrent motion, from End to End,
on green the white figures pass each other in pairs
to the huddle of darkness, and stop, and bend
to that logo of beast, fish, bird, inescapably theirs.

In the mind a bowl goes wide, curves in, and steals
through to neighbor the jack, and into fame:
Drake lets the Armada cool its Spanish heels.
Some games are old, and this is an old game.

Well, the tough tissue of chance is variously
confronted, concealed. And if one chooses
cushioning silence, surely this must be
the suavest idiom for Someone Loses.

The Woods

In this summer month, two separate men were lost
in the local woods. Can woods be local?
Is there more than one wood? It is unlikely.
Though there are two kinds of woods, visible, and not.

The first man was feeble-minded. Left
his goodwill party, saw something, heard
something, went to it. They found his body
later, after something wild found it first.

Fright, or starvation; or exposure. Woods
which are close and secret, practice exposure.
If he heard the cries, the dogs, the cries,
why didn't he answer? Why didn't they hear him?

Anyway the second man was strong-
minded as another; knew woods; went in alone.
They say never go in alone. But even in visible
woods, is that persuasive? They are interesting.

Even in high sun, they offer such levels
of shade—the tops of their tallest trees just stir
in the biggest wind. They are dark green to black
according to whether the light is sun or moon.

The second man was never found at all.
Never. So the people began to say he came out
somewhere, into sunlight or moonlight, for his own
purposes. But could the woods make him vanish?

The difference is, a visible wood stays put,
though it stirs and acts within itself. It is bounded.
The invisible wood stretches, arrives, and is there.
Going in alone is inevitable, unfortunately.

Also, dogs are forbidden, and silence enforced.
There is supposed to be a treasure, or witch, at the center.
But which, cannot be known, short of encounter.
And those lost, who return—and there are some—

cannot find the dictionary word to tell
how it went. If it's the treasure, they usually stay;
and if it's the witch, they can stay, too,
and she will send out a doppelgänger instead.

Another difference is that fewer are lost,
even temporarily, in the visible wood.
And another yet, that those broken or careless few
who are, are usually found; found in time.

The Blue-Eyed Exterminator

The exterminator has arrived. He has not intruded. He was summoned.
At the most fruitless spot, a regiment
of the tiniest of ants, obviously deluded,
have a jetty ferment of undisclosed intent.

The blue-eyed exterminator is friendly and fair;
one can tell he knows exactly what he is about.
He is young as the day that makes the buds puff out,
grass go rampant, big bees ride the air;

it seems the spring could drown him in its flood.
But though he appears modest as what he was summoned for,
he will prove himself more potent than grass or bud,
being a scion of the greatest emperor.

His success is total: no jet platoon on the wall.
At the door he calls good-bye and hitches his thumb.
For an invisible flick, grass halts, buds cramp, bees stall
in air. He has called, and what has been called has come.

The Limbo Dancer

No limbo this week. Or next. Now it turns out
the limbo dancer is dead. Tiles between sea
and bar are clean for the guests' uncertain feet
that search the band's racket for how they should move.
The sea is dark and those rungs of the moon's fire
lead nowhere; but broken and bright the ladder lies.

The limbo dancer had nutmeg-colored feet
with apricot-colored heels, and toes splayed out
inch and half-inch. The guests could barely see
that motion grip the tiles. And how can a man move
inch after half-inch, as his body lies
horizontal on air? In his teeth he carried fire.

When the rod was high (and there was no fire
yet) the limbo dancer addressed it: his feet
shifted in place, his pelvis jumped in, and out,
and the light from the sequins and sweat, that flies
over the ribs, showed how bone and muscle move.
His eyes shone, too, at whatever they managed to see.

The pans, sweet and metallic, that sent out
a torrent, hushed; and the dark drum, four feet
high, spoke, as the rod dropped into its last move.
The limbo dancer, tall, taller than drums, Watusi-
tall, beaten forward inch by inch, as inch relies
on inch-space, moved, moved: toes, heels, and fire.

Whatever more liquidly indifferent than the sea?
But the guests, diverted from rum and drawn by fire,
stared, as the head came under, and the great feet
shot up, the limbo dancer's flame put out
in his mouth's cavern. For a shocked space, the move
was into that joy where gravity's laws are lies.

The limbo dancer, together with his feet,
has disappeared, and the guests are put out.
In shadows, on sand, by the suddenly noisy sea,
the old foe gravity (plane, bird, poem) lies
in wait. If that stretched body fails to move,
who will kill gravity by inches, spring up, eat fire?

The limbo dancer's fire is certainly out.
The guests say, See, alas, he does not move.
But gravity lies beneath the dust of his feet.

Distance

Now loneliness enters the marrow
and she leaves the bed
to stare from midnight's window.

Around the steel of stars
that prick the nothingness
dark is absolute.

She calculates the where
but above all the when
of that light's departure

for the infinitesimal
target of her eye,
and sinks into that fall.

Softly to guard his sleep
she finds her lover's bed.
He has gone far and deep.

Only his body lies
innocent and lax.
She curves her own beside.

Where is he gone? Beneath
her touch, mysterious
moves his gentle breath

as, more mysterious, he goes
where she can never come
and where he cannot choose

the streets that he arranges
from familiar fragments
that lead him to strangers.

So they lie close and distant
as the starlight's origin
until she too departs

until in easy silence
sun floods, and covers
all secrets with its light.

The Thing about Crows

is, they are hoarse.
When you are hoarse, and shout,
you sound either desperate or ominous.
The crows are not desperate.

I say they are not desperate, but one flapped
desperately, dive-bombed this side, that,
by something tiny, with blue murder
and fury on its side.

It's a gentle day. Foliage shifts
gently in the air, and the buds on roses
puff out, and clouds maneuver and part
and meld in a gentle silence.
Now a crow goes heavily by, pounding
the air. Crows gather, gather, to shout
in their autumnal voices, hoarsely,
at the vulnerable spring.

The Shrivers

At dark three o'clock
with a grind and roar here
the garbage men come.

Faint light in her room
falls from the street lamp.
Where the room swam in hush

the scapegoat's sons, cleansers
of burden, come with chaos;
ply their ferocious

routine of salvation.
Her savior's violence
clangs in brute shocks

as what has turned broken,
disjointed, abandoned,
is sucked into limbo.

What it wishes to lose
and be loosed from lumbers
from the street that is shriven.

There are things here will go
in the same slam and crash.
Nor will she lie always

on the pillow's fresh surface,
hand curled at her cheek,
and wait for the wondrous

sluice of silence
that carries the blundering
laborious monster,

its unseen men clinging,
who erase time's disasters.
Without moving she lies

while the wings of great scavengers
pass over the roof toward
the hills of discard.

Loss of Sounds

Now lost, things a child heard,
without common value, weight
or provenance. Missed. Merely missed:

The ssshh, arithmetical
in time, perfect yes in correspondence
of two: the soft, soft soft soft-shoe.

The call early, from the early pony-
cart, red pompon, painted wheels:
fresh, free—ssh straw-str-aw berr-ies!

The peculiar far cry half wail
wailing, half threat, half summons,
fade, fail, from the night fast freight.

Sounds not replaceable. Deep
in the ear's memory, sounds. Hoc
est corpus meum.

Calling Collect

I have made the incantatory
gestures: the silver coin
the definition of an area, the numerals.

The coin has attracted a strange voice, a woman's.
I don't know her name, her face,
who she sleeps with, if anyone,

if she prays, or for what. She knows
none of these important things about me.
Our voices drop in each other's ears over March miles,

(country? gardens? thruways?); now she knows my name,
and yours. Will your voice accept my name? Yes.
I have been accepted by your voice.

"Who is that?" it might ask. Or say, "No, no
I can't possibly. I did, at one time, but not
now." Well, here you are, so far

away I could walk all day, or hitch, or run
and never reach you, passing through a map's
flower-colored states, past entire cities

tangled in their wires, in my hand
a crumpled address, and end in a diner
with a man swabbing the counter, ready to go home,

and he could say, "Oh that's another fifteen miles
from here, clear across town . . ." and when I
opened the ripped screen door again, an ambulance

could go he-hawing by, and the spring night blow
old papers round my ankles. But no,
even my silver coin falls back to me,

no silver required. You accept my call.
How melodramatic that sounds: You accept
my call! Well, that's what it is. For the love

of God let me hear your voice locate me.
Over distance, long, it is saying my name.
I speak to you.

The Gathering

Last night, first frost of sudden fall.
Hardiest of flowers fed by summertime
have survived; and the trees, in an arboreal May,
have bloomed, color for flower-color, as though light
sprang from the leaf in curious fulfill
ment, poising itself on a brittle brilliant surface.

Last night the dead walked through my sleep, light
handed, much beloved. I could perfectly identify each footfall
and certainly my lips have touched each face
that shone. They came freely as thirst to water, to fill
the dry cup. I choose to think about them in this time
of balance, having a process to consider while I may.

That loss of things which cannot, but do, fall
fall into boundless time—
which caused the furious dismay—
turns out now to show an altered face.
Compression, then distillation, have been used, to fill
what seemed shell: used ably, as wing uses the air for flight.

Perfectly true, the top of the hourglass is fill-
ing the needy bubble, and perfectly true of time—
gnaw, gnaw—that its honed teeth gnaw and deface:
the delicate edge blunted; the blood's loyal delight
sucked back; the trickle of sand falling, falling, do what you sullenly must or desperately may.

No question but what frost will have flower and leaf-fall.
It is not a matter of opposing frost or detaining May.
It is a matter of all your minutes which have secretly fill-
ed with leaf and cloud, voice, footfall and face.
It has no traffic with the handless clock of time:
it has to do with music, and marriage of shadow and light.

For something gathers, gathers: invisible, light,
soundless as cloud, delicate as the green fil-
ament of the leaf; full, as the waterfall
hangs motionless from the cliff's sustaining face.
This is what accumulates: it is what you may
hold, since out of the clutch of time.

You may keep this. Until there is nothing left to fill,
if a grain of sand, if a leaf fall, it does not fall into time
but falls before your face, from and into light.

The Fish Tank Room

It is the fish tank room—the small room
off the main corridor. In a minute or two
there will be December dusk. The tank is lit,
clean, bright, elegantly planted.
Before it sit three, silent as the fish.

From padded chairs they stare at the go and come,
the gorgeous trailings, the languorous beauties.
The lady in the purple cashmere sweater
is half smiling, as at indulged children.
The lady who is quite motionless

has her Cassandra eyes on an angel-
fish. The crooked man in gray looks
fixedly at the motion in the water,
the flash in that immaculate jungle.
Unlike the bulbs that glitter the tank

fuses are out in the heads attentively angled.
Now it is dimmer outside, but the motion continues:
the dart and nudge, the efficient glide,
the languid swerve. As night settles,
somewhere in the sweater's wearer,

in the dark-eyed head, in the sidewise leaner,
secrets are sealed, sealed; secrets
tiny and huge, frantic with silence,
more complex than the rich motions,
more light-filled than the darkening room

and more beautiful.

Noon

Peace the day says, and *peace.*
Seven colors sweep the palate sea.
A frigate bird cruises (look, no wings!)
only air currents. The fiddler crab,

sand-body from sand, pops up,
fiddles, dives back: grains of sand
fall after him. Exhibitionist,
the frigate bird cruises, sails, sails,

cruises. And *peace* and *peace*
says the fringe bubbling on the sand,
the sail just far enough to see.
Inside the wave, turquoise, violet,

green, cruise the cool fish, secret
but present. The human stares
in a trance of colored peace.
The dog lies in a stupor of sun,

and gently the sea-almond lets fall
one bright leaf to the sea. The frigate
bird drops: dives: rises:
and the cool fish sails too, sails

sails high in its blistering air.

Tears

Tears leave no mark on the soil
or pavement; certainly not in sand
or in any known rain forest;
never a mark on stone.
One would think that no one in Persepolis
or Ur ever wept.

You would assume that, like Alice,
we would all be swimming, buffeted
in a tide of tears.
But they disappear. Their heat goes.
Yet the globe is salt
with that savor.

The animals want no part in this.
The hare both screams and weeps
at her death, one poet says.
The stag, at death, rolls round drops
down his muzzle; but he is in
Shakespeare's forest.

These cases are mythically rare.
No, it is the human being who persistently
weeps; in some countries, openly, in others, not.
Children who, even when frightened, weep most hopefully;
women, licensed weepers.
Men, in secret, or childishly; or nobly.

Could tears not make a sea of their mass?
It could be salt and wild enough;
it could rouse storms and sink ships,
erode, erode its shores:
tears of rage, of love, of torture,
of loss. Of loss.

Must we see the future
in order to weep? Or the past?
Is that why the animals
refuse to shed tears?
But what of the present, the tears of the present?
The awful relief, like breath

after strangling? The generosity
of the verb "to shed"?
They are a classless possession
yet are not found in the museum
of even our greatest city.
Sometimes what was human, turns
into an animal, dry-eyed.

Only Alice

      entered that brilliant intimate
room; you cannot, ever, pick
the grapes whose luster mounds the plate
or hear that gilt French clock tick.

Will not smell the red roses, ever;
taste, touch or hear. Only your eyes
watch eyes which see the face you never
will. That room is silent with surprise

and lure of inaccessible terrain.
The gilded frame surrounds a whole
of something present that explains
the old belief that it can snatch a soul.

It shows no welcome, and no malice,
ambiguous as any Mona Lisa.
You are outside. There is no talis-
man; no passport and no visa.

So stare and stay; so stare, beguiled
and balked. And there's the matter
of luck, should you know—like a furious child—
that what you may not enter, you can shatter.

First Woman

Do animals expect spring?
Ground hard as rancor,
wind colder than malice.
Do they think that will change?

Sky no color and low;
grass is no color, and trees
jerk in the bitter gust.
In this air nothing flies.

Do they believe it will change,
grass be soft and lustrous,
rigid earth crack
from the push of petals,

sky retreat into blue,
the red wide rose breathe
summer, and the butterfly
err on sweet air?

First woman, Lucy, or another,
did you know it all waited
somewhere to come back?
On the first stripped, iron day

did you believe that?
On this merciless morning
I wake, first woman,
with what belief?

Figure

For William Meredith

Out of the bone landscape
of stone and sand, a man
on a burro appears

alone, distant;
egg for head, stick arms,
stick legs, out of all years

of the sand, the stone; going
to no seen spot, confers
a human form on the eye

before he vanishes
as though bony distance
had eaten him.

Nothing is like him. Vulnerable,
he has not profited
from the feral faunal data:

the yellow crab spider
on golden rod; the brown
beetle on soil; the katy-

did on its green leaf;
the delectable Viceroy
mimicking the acrid Monarch. Outwit,

or lie low and wait. The cockroach, in 300 million
years has not seen fit

to change. Yet durability
cannot be said
to be all. Nor fear.

The stony bony sandy view
shifted itself, focused
upon him till he left it there.

Reading on the Beach

What time is it? Raphael, says Vasari,
"showed himself sweet and pleasant . . ."
In the big Caribbean day, on the small
foxed page, those hours of paint and gold
are here. The boy is a detail: this morning
Raphael commences the boy holding a scroll.

Compulsively the Caribbean's rim
collapses over the rumpled sand: fall,
steal, hush; tide punctual in a blue
overlaid by violet; tide on time
as the machine in the chest counts and counts.
The boy Raphael imagined does not breathe.

This is *now. Then* can mean Raphael,
or future, as "perhaps then we shall . . ."
The Chimera was steadfast, compared with time's
aspects. Its undependability
is legendary: the prisoner's monster,
the saint's cipher. Perhaps does not exist.

Raphael Sanzio of Urbino was
"as excellent as gracious," Vasari says,
"with a natural modesty and goodness." (He says, too,
"Most artists have hitherto displayed something
of folly and savagery.") For a detail on the high
altar of Aracoeli, Raphael did a boy with a scroll

looking up at the Virgin. "For his beautiful
face and well-proportioned limbs he cannot
be surpassed." What of the boy, and the foam's
semicircle that slides and winks? Time
in some sort of weather took Vasari's hand.

Raphael's boy stares the centuries down
as Raphael's hand though dust is manifest.
Sea goes too far back to imagine,
forward too far even for Raphael's boy.
On its edge is the boy of Raphael's hand.
On Vasari's foxed page my hand is warm.

Hourglass

"Flawless" is the word, no doubt, for this third of May
that has landed on the grounds of Mayfair,
the Retirement Community par excellence.

Right behind the wheels of the mower, grass
explodes again, the bare trees most tenderly
push out their chartreuse tips.

Bottle bees are back. Feckless, reckless,
stingless, they probably have a function.
Above the cardinal, scarlet on the rim

of the birdbath, twinning himself,
they hover, cruise the flowers, mate.
The tiny water catches the sky.

On the circular inner road, the lady
untangles the poodle's leash from her cane.
He is wild to chase the splendid smells.

The small man with the small smile,
rapidly steering his Amigo,
bowls past. She would wave, but can't.

All around, birds and sexual flowers
are intent on color, flight, fragrance.
The gardener sweeps his sweaty face

with a khaki sleeve. His tulips are shined
black at their centers. They have come along nicely.
He is young and will be gone before dark.

The man in the Amigo has in mind a May
a mirror of this, but unobtainable
as the touch of the woman in that glass.

The sun's force chills him. But the lady
with the curly poodle could melt her cane
in the very heat of her precious pleasure.

She perfectly understands the calendar
and the sun's passage. But she grips the leash
and leans on the air that is hers and here.

JOSEPHINE JACOBSEN has published seven books of poetry, two of criticism with William R. Mueller, and three collections of short fiction. During a career that spans seventy years, she has been a regular contributor to periodicals such as *Commonweal, The Kenyon Review, The Nation, The New Yorker,* and *Poetry.*

Jacobsen's many awards include the Lenore-Marshall Award for the best book of poetry published the previous year, for *The Sisters;* a Fellowship from the Academy of American Poets for service to poetry; the selection of *On the Island: Short Stories* as one of the five nominees for the PEN-Faulkner fiction award; and, most recently, the Shelley Award of the Poetry Society of America (1993).

Jacobsen served two terms as poetry consultant to the Library of Congress. She was inducted into the American Academy of Arts and Letters in 1994.

She lives in Baltimore with her husband, Eric Jacobsen.

LIBRARY OF CONGRESS CATALOGING-IN-PUBLICATION DATA

Jacobsen, Josephine.
    In the crevice of time : new and collected poems / Josephine Jacobsen.
       p.   cm. — (Johns Hopkins, poetry and fiction)
    ISBN 0-8018-5116-5 (acid-free paper)
      I. Title.   II. Series.
PS3519.A42415 1995
811'.54—dc20   95-2798